GAS TANK & OTHER STORIES

GAS TANK

& Other Stories

Dennis E. Bolen

ANVIL PRESS PUBLISHERS

Printed and bound in Canada
First Edition
Cover design: JT Osborne
Cover photo: Dirk Beck
Author portrait: Maurice Spira

The publisher gratefully acknowledges the assistance of the
B.C. Arts Council and the Canada Council for the Arts.

THE CANADA COUNCIL | LE CONSEIL DES ARTS
FOR THE ARTS | DU CANADA
SINCE 1957 | DEPUIS 1957

Canadian Cataloguing in Publication Data

Bolen, Dennis E. (Dennis Edward), 1953-
Gas tank & other stories

ISBN 1-895636-15-9
I. Title
PS8553.04755G37 1997   C813'.54   C97-910201-4
PR9199.3.B577G37 1997

'The Fatality' was previously published in *The Canadian Fiction Magazine*.
'Toba Inlet' appeared in *Introductions From An Island*, University of Victoria Press.

Represented in Canada by the Literary Press Group
Distributed by General Distribution Services

Anvil Press
Suite 204-A — 175 East Broadway,
Vancouver, BC
Canada   V5T 1W2

For

Alexei Yashin

Thanks a million, pal.

Contents

The Fatality

It was just as he had described it. The motorcycle was all over the place and in the lights of the car I could see glints of chrome pieces scattered over the road in the distance. Halvorsen was in the ditch just as the driver had said, with his head propped up on the mailbag he'd been carrying. Dad was turning the car so I could see how bad he was. When the lights came I knew we would have a hard time keeping this man alive.

My father called through the wind and rain: "How is he?"

"Not good. Fractured skull, I think."

"Well, let's get him in the car. I hope he don't die before we get him down, the paperwork's a bastard."

"Yeah, well, just let's get him out of here and don't talk like that." In those years the old man had a bad attitude about our role as provisional lifesavers. "He might stand a chance if you don't keep standing around complaining."

"Okay, just because you're gettin' to be bigger than me and you got some kinda education don't mean you can mouth off like that to your old man."

"I can say anything I want but I got more concern for this guy right now." I spread a blanket close to Halvorsen and began easing him onto it. He sensed my moving him and started to moan. "Look, he's coming out of it. Gimme a hand, eh?" The moans turned to gasps and he struggled weakly. The blood showing at his ears started to run and his eyes opened, showing only the whites.

"He's damn bad. You better drive good and fast this time."

"I'll drive like I damn well feel like."

With both of us holding the blanket we eased Halvorsen into the back of the station wagon.

Driving down the mountain, Halvorsen mumbled and groaned with the bumps in the road. At a bad stretch he started yelling and struggled to get up.

"For chrissake hold him down or he'll have us all in a goddamn wreck!"

"He can't do nothin'." I leaned back and tried to steady him. He cramped violently and hit his head on the roof of the car. The bleeding from his ears got worse amid the screeching.

"He's not goin' to make it." Dad's voice was soft for the first time since we'd been interrupted at the dinner table.

"For once I agree with you."

Halvorsen quieted down after that and we made it to the hospital with him faintly breathing.

On the way out of town we stopped at an all-night restaurant and drank cups of coffee.

This was before the ambulance service was extended to most rural areas and that was the last accident we went to that year. With autumn and cooler weather the traffic dropped off and the resort business slowed to a trickle. Winter rains washed the motorcycle skid-marks until they were just a memory. News wasn't something we sought after with any great vigour in those days and we didn't hear about how Halvorsen was doing until about Christmas, when the replacement mail carrier stopped in at the café one afternoon.

"Say, you know that fella you guys picked up down the road last fall?" Just my Dad was at the counter to listen, but I heard the man from where I was in back.

"Yeah. How'd he do, anyway?"

"The fellas in the yard were sayin' the other day that he'd been in town and talked to one of 'em. He got over the head injury, you know."

"Uh huh." Dad's usual tone hadn't changed though I could sense his interest. He took a long drag on his cigarette. The smoke curled around his head and fouled a ray of sunlight passing through the window, casting a dirty sort of light on the counter.

"Had family trouble after he got out of the hospital. Heard his wife ran off. Couldn't stand life with a changed man is the way I heard it."

"Wouldn't doubt."

"She took the kids, house and everything. He's workin' light duty at the dockyards now." The man downed his coffee and got up to leave. "I heard he's gone kinda funny. Weird in the head."

"Wouldn't doubt," said Dad.

My father didn't say anything to me about what he'd learned and it didn't matter to me since I'd heard it all anyway. The rest of the winter passed with us hearing only the occasional word about the misfortunes of a rejected man.

Summer came late and business was slow all spring. One day I was standing in the kitchen wrapping an order for one of the cabins. The café door slammed and I heard my father greet a man louder than usual. I leaned over a bit so I could see through the serving counter. A man with long hair over his forehead and a light summer jacket was sitting at the counter talking to Dad. I recognized Halvorsen only after he removed his hat and looked through at me. His eyes were clear but they had a peculiar look to them and I turned away after a moment, uncomfortable and wondering why.

"How ya been doin'." My father was unusually enthusiastic. He usually didn't talk to people with much interest unless it had to do with hockey. Since it wasn't hockey season I decided to move closer and listen in.

"Not bad, " Halvorsen said. "I'm not too bad these days."

"What you doin' for a living now? Heard you were workin' at the dockyards."

"I'm finished that now."

"Gonna take it easy for a while?"

"I'm headin' up the road. Gonna start over."

At this my Dad just nodded. He never was one to pry too much into another man's life. He'd already asked more questions than I'd ever heard him ask. Things were silent for a while.

Then Dad piped up again. "Got anything particular in mind?"

"Sure do." Halvorsen's voice was just audible as I stepped out the back door to deliver the order. When I got back to the café he was about to leave. I could see him standing by the door, still talking to my old man. His voice was soft. The way he looked made me wonder where he was heading and what he was going to do when he got there. When he left I watched through a side window as he opened the door of a fairly new red coupe and climbed in. A while later Dad came into the kitchen and started cutting sandwich meat. He often came back to work if the café was empty.

"Go over and tell your Mother we're goin' into town in a while. Ask her if she needs anything."

"You goin' too?" I wasn't used to him tagging along on my supply trips. He seldom left Mom alone to run the place herself. "Who's going to mind the counter?"

"We'll close up. I don't expect to be gone long."

About an hour later we started off. I drove while Dad sat and looked out the window and smoked. We approached the dangerous section of the road and I slowed down. In years of driving on the mountain we had been lucky enough to stay out of trouble and I took no chances. As we came around a hairpin turn I saw a red speck out on one of the viewpoints far below. They were more for emergency stops than viewing the scenery so I wondered if there might be trouble.

"I think I'll pull up and have a look over there."

The old man was detached as usual. "Suit yourself."

We stopped along the side of the highway. The car was parked with its front wheels against the guard rail. No one was in sight.

"People don't usually park that close to the edge."

"No." Dad held on to his disinterested tone, even though we both could see that things were not as they should have been. "Well, get goin'," he growled. "We got other business too, you know."

I got out of the truck and crossed over the road onto the soft gravel shoulder. Before reaching the car I saw the black hose connected to the end of the exhaust pipe and where it entered the passenger compartment through a semi-closed side-vent. The motor was running and Halvorsen was slumped behind the wheel. The driver's door was locked. I hunted around for a rock to break a window. There were plenty around but it took a long time. I had trouble gripping them in my hands. Finally I trapped a large boulder in my arms and cracked the driver's side window. The glass was tough, I hurt my arm reaching in to unlock the door. Halvorsen's neck was cold and hard to the touch. There was a note perched on the spokes of the steering wheel.

I should have died last year . . .

I didn't read the rest. After turning off the ignition I headed back to the truck.

"Christ if he didn't go and kill himself!"

The truck seemed to start on its own and I headed it back onto the road.

At the bottom of the mountain we had to stop for a cow standing in the middle of the road. A young boy was desperately trying to get her to move on. The old cow just stared at us with large black eyes, calm. I gazed straight ahead with whitened knuckles on the wheel.

"His fingernails were blue." There was a dryness I found difficult to talk through.

My old man just sat there and smoked and didn't say anything.

Fight

A soldier has a four-inch shard of glinting-grey metal stuck in his shoulder. Its needle point has penetrated the bone near the joint, rear entry, and looks like a miniature thunderbolt thrown by a god.

The godly eruption came as he turned his back. A surprise, he thinks.

My first shell.

Wish I'd seen it.

The pinprick hurts like fire. The soldier reaches to it, fingers and tugs on it, winces to the painflash. The shard holds fast.

It hurts, but . . . this isn't so bad.

"Richard! You think the sergeant's dead? You think he's dead back there?"

"I got a chunk of shell in my shoulder."

"They gotta be dead."

"Sure they do, but I gotta get this thing out of my shoulder."

"You hurt bad? You think the sergeant's dead?"

"Look, what's your name? Charles, Charlie?" The soldier looks up. "I got a piece of iron sticking in me and I can't get it out. That's what's concerning me right now. As for the sergeant, you saw him go, and the others too. They went over there and the shell came and stuck me in the back of the shoulder and they, all of them, your pal Stu, the sergeant and that other kid, I don't know his name . . . "

"Christopher . . ."

"Christopher. They disappeared and we haven't seen them again. They're not calling to us. Chances are they're all gone. You put it together. I got a slice of Fritz's metal-work sticking out of me. Help me with it for gosh sakes or go look for what's left of the sergeant if there is any but stop standing there whining, will you? Help me get this thing out . . . "

Charlie squashes through the mud around where Richard leans against the trench wall, holding on to a piece of lumber set as a foothold in the damp earth. He begins to help Richard with his first wound.

This isn't so bad, thinks Richard. You get the first one out of the way, the rest can't scare ya. That's the way it feels. He grips the wood, part of the steps to the top of the trench, thinking he might fall. Charlie touches the metal protruding out of Richard. Blood colours the khaki around the wound. Charlie prepares to yank the shrapnel out. Richard holds himself, closes his eyes.

He waits, expecting torture. Nothing happens.

Richard opens his eyes and sees Charlie shrinking back and the tears running down his face and knows he will have to find a dressing station.

"You think maybe the sergeant and the other guys made it?" Charlie utters through his anguish.

"See for yourself."

The crying man looks again. "They're not there now."

"No, they're not there."

"Maybe they're somewhere else."

"Go and see."

"You don't mind me leavin' you?"

"No. I'm fine. Just got a shard of steel in my shoulder, as you can see."

"Sorry I can't get it out for you."

"Probably best. I should find a dressing station."

"Where?"

"Somewhere."

"I'll go over and find the sergeant."

"You do that."

Charlie stumbles down the trench, past the dugout opening. Richard watches him climb through the shell crater, still steaming, that did the damage to his aching shoulder and made the others disappear. Charlie goes out of sight around the bend.

Some far-off explosions begin to be not so far off. Charlie reappears down the trench, his shoulders hunched in disappointment. Richard feels another pain from his metal appendage, a vibration, like a drill-bit boring deeper into his bone. The air is vibrating. He ungrips the foot-hold and sits flatly in the mud, covering his ears and face. A shell hits the top of the trench overtop the dugout. Then the noise subsides and Richard hears the scream. Or screams, he cannot discern how many. A sound he quickly banishes with hands to his ears before his heart explodes with the pity of it, the unearthly terror.

When Richard can again see down the trench Charlie is lying on his back, a little off-centre from the duckboards.

Richard cannot see specific wounds, but by the way the body splays, face sagging, hands outstretched and curled, he knows Charlie is dead.

That's the way it is, he thinks.

He is almost glad for the pain. There is no grief, only strange bitterness. At the least, after two months of training, weeks of travel overland and by ocean liner, and six hours of trench duty, Richard is glad to be a veteran.

On the way back to the dressing station, Richard crossed the headquarters area.

"Private!"

"Sir?"

"Aren't you supposed to be in the sap position? Where is your sergeant?"

"Dead, sir."

"Dead? How?"

"A shell sir."

"There are no shells, Private, we have intelligence that there are no shells landing in your sector."

"I saw them, sir."

"Learn to follow orders, Private. It's the only way you'll survive this experience. There are no shells."

Richard spoke an answer to the officer, who was English, but did not make himself loud enough to be heard over the near-distant artillery rumble. The officer, a major, glared at him. A young lieutenant approached.

"Shells landing in C sector, sir." The lieutenant handed the major a paper.

Hardening eyes flitted for a moment to the paper, then back to Richard.

"There are shells landing in your sector."

"Yes, sir."

"Are you wounded?"

"Yes, sir."

"Then off with you to hospital."

"Yes, sir."

Richard went.

The major examined the paper closely.

"Your men need discipline, Lieutenant."

"Yes, sir."

The major handed the paper back. The lieutenant took it, smiling, respectful.

A doctor spent several minutes prying the shard from Richard's shoulder with an aged pair of pliers.

"We can't help you for the pain, lad. I'm sorry."

Richard ground his teeth. When he'd gone to the recruiting office to sign up, there were men as fit as he who were turned down because of flat feet, bent fingers, missing teeth. They took Richard.

Perfect, he must have been. Perfect, now with a hole in his shoulder. Perfect. The doctor dressed the wound.

"Light duty for two weeks, Private. Take it easy."

The doctor scribbled a chit and handed it to him. Richard wrestled his tunic on and took the chit with his good hand.

Outside the tent, struggling to keep his rifle properly presented, the late February wind off the plains lifted the unbuttoned lapels of his tunic and made him shiver.

That's it, no more holes. No more punctures in this skin-less-than-perfect.

The persistent boom of far-off guns mixed with the wind-sounds in his ears.

I swear to God!

Richard found Lieutenant Speckley coming from the Company Headquarters trench.

"Richard, you should steer clear of the major. He's pretty stiff."

"All right."

"All right sir, Richard."

"Aw, come on, Jason . . . "

"You can't call me by my first name here."

"Yes, sir."

"Anyway, the major wants you to come along now, and do a recon."

"Where?"

"Back to the sap. He wants to see for himself."

"Let him go."

"You don't understand. Orders."

"You're right. I don't understand."

A line of soldiers a dozen strong, with two officers, entered the sap trench. The major walked to the ruined dugout.

"Lieutenant," he barked, "have this cleared."

"Yes, sir."

A nearby shell-hit rained dirt upon them.

"Quickly."

"Yes, sir."

"And where is that man who was here?"

"Private Delta, sir. I'll get him."

The major strode toward the heavenward-staring body of Charlie.

Lieutenant Speckley and Richard approached and stood aside while the major brushed dirt from a wooden step in the trench. He wielded his field telescope.

"I wouldn't do that, sir. The sergeant did that just—"

"Lieutenant! Silence this man and instruct him in the proper protocol."

"Private Delta. Speak when spoken to."

"Yes, sir."

The Major stiffly climbed steps and swung his telescope to rest on the parapet. After a long look he spoke in a low growl to the younger men below.

"There is little to see here and much to do . . . "

The shriek of falling iron erased the rest of the major's words. The dugout took five shells in ten seconds. Several more hit forward of the trench, sending debris in a horizontal flying canopy over their heads. The atmosphere went dark. Richard and Lieutenant Speckley crouched themselves tiny in the mud.

Five more shells hit in a pattern around the trench, cutting off the two groups of men. Then a lull. Richard looked up. The lieutenant, newer than Richard to this, kept his eyes covered.

All Richard could see was the major, lying where a shell-blast had sent him, leaning against the opposite wall of the trench. Though the man now had no face, Richard noticed that the telescope was still intact.

Down the trench, through the clearing smoke and dust, Richard could see no indication there had been men with them when this had started.

Gone, he thought. Seems natural. You stand in the rain, you get wet.

Lieutenant Speckley shivered beside him. A few more shells came down, back of the trench, going away. Richard relaxed his crouch, letting the blood run in him again. A strange sound came from somewhere.

"What's that?" Lieutenant Speckley stared through reddened eyes at Richard.

"Voices . . . "

It came to Richard in a cold terrible feeling in his throat.

"Raiding party! They're coming. We gotta get out of here."

Richard rose, swinging his rifle.

"Wait!" Lieutenant Speckley spoke up. Richard spared one second to look at him before he took flight. The look on the officer's face suggested he felt he should be doing something different than an enlisted man, but couldn't decide what. "The others . . . "

"Take care of themselves." Richard gripped Speckley's arm and tugged. "It's an attack, Jason!"

"I know, I know . . . "

The lieutenant looked around for the first time and jolted from Richard's grip when he discerned the ragged hanging flesh of the major's head. "Oh God . . . "

"Come on!" Richard tugged again at the man's tunic.

They ran down the trench. The dugout area was a fleshy nightmare.

"Christ!"

"Never mind."

The peculiar whine of approaching attackers, crazy-sounding and unearthly, was a present thing now. It made the muscles in Richard's neck feel like steel rods. He felt the power that fear can confer and knew instantly it could kill him or save him, depending on how he used it.

"The communication trench!" Jason Speckley seemed now to have found his leadership instinct. His words came to Richard near-choking.

"No," Richard called. "They'll bomb it. Over the top

first, then into the trench." He knew not where the words came from but felt what years later he would know to be a psychic sense of what to do, as if the thoughts and intentions of the attacking troops, now only two hundred yards away, were his for the reading. Without further words he grabbed the Lieutenant's arm and hauled him onto the mound of the fallen dugout. The officer followed without hesitation. Exposed, they ran.

It felt good to let loose in open territory for a change, instead of always having to scramble in mucky trenches, around objects, men, soft parts and corners. Here was the freedom something like a breakaway in a soccer game with the ball coming along nicely in front and everybody sweating and straining impossibly behind. Richard heard noises above the wind in his ears and thought he saw the earth twitch around them. His instinct made him weave, duck and jump.

In thirty seconds they were at another trench and flew down into the mud, gasping. Richard looked back over the parapet. Little clots of grey appeared for a second at the lip of the sap trench and dropped out of sight. He sank back to where Speckley puffed, gaining his breath. When he could say anything the words did not sound for Richard above the impact of more artillery, which he imagined was sighted on their recent field run, pounding along the open ground toward their cover-place.

The fatal knowledge hit Richard again—a sense from nowhere—and at the same instant he remembered his hopeful thought of hours ago: no more holes in this skin. He felt strange. In the silence of crashing noise he locked eyes with Speckley, grabbed his arm again and ran down the trench toward the back-running communication route.

It's like talk. Talk in my brain.

Richard wondered how he would explain it if he ever tried. He might try with Jason, if he ever got off this 'officer' stuff.

They made it to the communication trench as the artillery found their former resting spot. They ran stumbling down the shallow route, ramming fists into the soft walls to steady themselves at the frequent turns.

A particularly wide shell-crater stopped them as the absence of running sounds behind them made it less urgent to run headlong.

Richard swung his rifle to the parapet and had a look back. No grey dots. He sank back and looked at Speckley.

"It's all right, I think."

"All right . . . "

"We better figure out where we are, though."

"Right. I think we're almost back to headquarters."

"We took a different trench. This one goes to the right."

"We did?"

"Yeah."

"Oh . . . "

"This one seems to go parallel a bit."

"Can we find our own trench?"

"I don't know."

"I should know."

"How can you?"

"I don't know, I just should."

"Well, reason would suggest it's got to be somewhere to the left."

"That's reasonable."

"But it means going over open ground again. I don't know . . . "

"Where does this trench lead?"

"How should I know?"

"I was hoping . . . but I guess we better do something."

"You better do something. You're the officer."

"You've been up here more than me."

"Six hours more."

"Well, that's something."

"Maybe. Got a hole in my shoulder."

"Does it hurt?"

"Some."

"Sorry."

"Nothing you can do about it. Major doesn't care."

"Not any more."

"Yeah, how 'bout that."

"That was ugly."

"I think you better get used to it."

Speckley rose from the shell-crater and crawled upward to peer in the direction from which they'd come. "Doesn't look like anybody's out there." His voice was hopeful.

"No, but there is."

Speckley dropped back down and picked at a clod of dirt near his hand. Richard watched him as he tried to rub the grime away between his thumb and fingers. The lieutenant looked up. "Not much like home, huh?"

"Naw," Richard drawled. "A little maybe. In the cleared parts."

"No trees. Not like we have."

"Trees are a big asset around here. Something you're proud to own. Our trees are a pain. Everywhere. Can't see anything for all the trees . . . "

"I wouldn't mind seeing some of them right now."

"Yeah, I guess . . . "

"We have to find our trench."

"No. There's no point. We'll get seen out there and get killed."

"We can't stay here."

"Of course we can't, but we can keep going back." Richard gestured with his head. "The Australians are over here, aren't they?"

"French. The Australians are on the other side."

"French then, so what?"

"So what? We must find our own lines."

"We will, once we're back there."

"Right now." Speckley's voice rose. It occurred to Richard that he was remembering his rank again. "We've got to warn of the attack."

"It's just a patrol raid. They know by now."

"Not everything."

"So what, it was just a skirmish. They're not coming all the way."

"Headquarters will want to counter-attack."

"Oh goody."

"We go, now." Lieutenant Speckley pointed. "Over that way."

"It's wrong. I'm telling you."

"It's an order, sorry."

"Shove it."

"Come on, Richard. I covered for you with the major."

"He got killed, so what?"

"He wanted to put you on report."

"For what? Telling the truth?"

"The truth is sometimes against orders. You don't follow orders very well."

"I'll follow them if they're right."

Speckley laughed, getting up.

"I'm going. You can come or not."

"You're crazy."

Richard stepped aside as Speckley scrambled to the parapet and climbed up to look toward the enemy lines. "There's no sign of them."

"Not until you start running there won't be."

Richard looked up at the officer. Speckley's face was hard when he turned it. Richard ignored him and stepped up to see for himself. He was awed by the openness of the ground around them.

"Regardless . . ." Speckley muttered and scrambled to the lip of the crater. He was gone across the broken farmland in an instant. Richard watched him go.

Crazy. I know he'll get it. He's running too straight.

Richard studied the disappearing officer—the movement, the stumbles over difficult terrain.

He'll die, moving like that.

Movement. It came clear to him. Richard shouldered his rifle and leapt out of the hole.

Step here, step there, don't go in there.

A mortar shell descended on Richard's route, showering him, but sending most of its flinging razor-blade harvest drilling into soft ground. Well ahead of him Speckley ran headlong. Another shell descended. Richard saw the other man falter, then renew his pace.

They ran on.

Sharp cracks, rifle-fire, came in through the increasing mortar drop. Richard became more and more selective of where he let his feet go. He saw Speckley totter again and nearly fall. As Richard reached him, he was struggling to regain his pace, gripping his lower back.

"You're hit!" Richard got a hand under Speckley's armpit.

"So?" Amid the deadly atmosphere Richard was amazed he noticed the fact that Speckley's voice sounded ridiculous. The man is still operating on the idea an officer had to say something.

A rattle sound came over the field. Richard saw immediately the stitch-work of machine-gun bullets wrinkling the ground to one side. Richard still felt he knew where to step but was uncertain of what to do with Speckley. They ran on.

The noise behind them increased. Richard's hand was slippery with blood from supporting Speckley, whose strength and determination to go on strangely affected him. Despite his disdain for officiousness, Richard began to feel sentimental about the man. Dodging bullets, he made up his mind that both of them would pull through this thing. His hand felt the jolt and he knew the lieutenant had been hit again. Speckley tripped face-down in the mud, blood gouting from a shoulder.

Struggling to pick him up, Richard noted clearly for the first time the trench they sought, twenty yards ahead. Hoisting the injured man he tramped heavily forward.

On the lip of the trench, as Richard prepared to leap into cover, a last mortar shell blew up behind them. Richard felt the metal hit his load and Speckley yelped. They fell into the trench.

Richard landed with Speckley on top of him and in his exhaustion could not move for a moment. He saw two privates huddled not far away, the barrage having apparently interrupted their task of laying telephone wire. They approached cautiously, heads down. One of them pulled the wounded officer off Richard.

"Holy . . . "

Richard emerged from the dust and the blood, rearranged his rifle and straightened his aching shoulders.

Steam from the stew filled his face, moved like a soft hand across his forehead. Richard wavered above the bowl, enjoying. Forgetting. In the corner of the dugout, away from him, three soldiers were chatting merrily.

"Me, I'm from Saskatoon. Good place to be from, I'll tell ya . . . "

"Better'n here, I'd say. You?"

"Toronto. This place is strange to me."

"Just like home if you're from Barrie. You never get out of town much?"

"Naw. Workin' all the time."

"Like it here?"

"Naw, it's strange."

"'T's not so strange as it's flat and open, y'know? Like it's just askin' to have a war on it. Too easy to move around without roads. Back home you could get all these fellas lost on your average farm . . . "

"Who'd fight over Saskatchewan?"

"I seen men do it . . . "

"Toronto they fight over where the buses stop."

"Huh . . . ?"

Laughter. They ate and chattered.

Richard sat, enjoying the steam on his face. Hunger was like acid inside him. He wanted to eat but loathed the idea of losing the gentle steam-hand upon his face.

"Say, there . . . " One of the kibitzers turned across to Richard. "Where you hail from?"

Richard looked up. "Me?"

"Yeah . . ." By Richard's account, it was Toronto who had spoken to him. "Kinda quiet, aren't ya?"

"Yeah."

"So? Where you from?"

The soldiers chewed their stew, looking at him. Richard watched them eat, remembered his hunger and took a bite.

"Unsociable are ya?"

Richard chewed. The taste was like paper, somewhat metallic. He looked into his bowl but the dim candlelight of the dugout did not allow him to see the food. His hand had a stripe of Jason's blood across it where he had failed to wash. His uniform was soaked with it, drying and getting stiff. The food, he realized, tasted like blood. He gagged.

"Hey!"

Toronto was beginning to show annoyance.

"Uh . . ." Richard stirred in his chair, nearly glad now to be required to speak instead of eat. "I'm from Nanaimo. On Vancouver Island. That's over the other end of the country from . . . "

"I know where the hell Nanaimo is, chum."

Richard stared at the man, trying not to taste the food still in his mouth.

"Whatcha do for a livin' there in Nanaimo?"

"I was a miner."

"A miner."

"Aye."

"Diggin' for gold?"

"Coal."

"A miner," piped the man from Saskatoon. "Course you're a minor, you can't hardly be eighteen!"

Laughter.

An officer appeared at the burlap curtain. "Delta? Which one is Private Delta?"

"Here," Richard said.

"You'll be reassigned tomorrow, son, since most of your unit seems to be lost."

"Yes, sir."

"And your lieutenant. Speckley . . . He's pretty bad."

"Yes, sir."

The officer was a middle-aged captain. Probably a reservist, Richard thought. In real life maybe an accountant with a practice in some small cozy town.

"He's a brave man . . ." The older man regarded Richard closely. "Leading you across the open like that. Sorry, son."

"Yes, sir."

The captain left.

The soldiers ate. Richard, forgetting the taste of blood, ate.

"Another miner bites the dust," said Toronto.

Richard hated the mines. In fact he'd only been down once, the day before he enlisted. Though he loved and admired his father, Richard Delta Jr. was confounded to know how the old man had withstood twenty years of underground work. Though he never asked, Richard always thought his father had some natural talent for it, some innate property for discomfort and the overcast doom of the mile-down coal shaft. If so, the genes had not been passed along. Richard spent the slow hours of his first and only shift hugging his knees in a dark spur, in the charge of a mine old-hand who knew the signs—the wild-eyed fear and closed in privacy of the claustrophobic just before he cracks.

The kind man covered for young Richard all day and gently escorted him to the top at quitting time, saying goodbye with meaning.

The war seemed a fresh diversion after that. Richard was eager. Not so much to see the world or fight the Hun, but to board a ship to take him far away from the black mouth of a coal shaft.

The next morning, six weeks after his arrival in Belgium and his first experience with the war, Richard, the sole survivor of Squad One from the Nanaimo Expeditionary Detachment of October 1914 was assigned to another sapper's post. This time, horror of horrors, a tunneling detail. The only saving grace was the relative absence of officers. They disdained getting their uniforms dirty. The smell was bad too, with infrequent breathing holes. And strangely, after seeing the coal mine owner's son cut to steaming strips with flying metal while riding on his own back, Richard did not mind the solid gloom of the underground. No claustrophobia at all.

Musta had it scared out of me.

At least one good thing had come out of that first terrible taste of action.

The detail was charged with burrowing under four hundred yards of no-mans-land to a forward observation post.

Once the digging was finished, the good part was crawling out among the low scrub and heaved ground to observe enemy movements, listening for troops and heavy machinery. The sergeant of the 'Tunnel Rats', as they liked to call themselves, was a jovial man named Ralph who, at age twenty-seven, out-aged his average private by six years. He enjoyed his command, establishing cozy quarters underground where scant officer or enemy attention ever bothered the air of private mission each man had: to get through this unpleasant experience the best, most comfortable way possible. Ralph seemed to support this effort and had what he considered a damn good crew for the purpose.

Best among them he had to admit was Private Richard Delta, the reluctant former miner from British Columbia.

"Richard!"

"Yes, Ralph."

"Could you see that the tobacco comes down with today's rations?"

"Surely."

"Go up there yourself and make sure they don't short us like last time."

"You can depend on me."

"I know I can, but be careful up there. When officers are around you have to salute. Salute them all. Sir after everything. Remember last time?"

"Yes, Ralph."

"It took some talking. I don't want to lose my best possum."

"Nope."

"Good then. Get going."

Richard moved back along the tunnel to where the entrance lay in a forward trench. A few of the soldiers posted there looked disinterestedly his way. The sector was a quiet one, a welcome to Richard, who knew more than anyone around him what it was like when it wasn't quiet.

With a minimum of officer-contact, Richard managed to round up the supplies and head back to the tunnel without trouble. He carried the all-important tobacco ration in a large pouch inside his tunic. Rounding a slow curve in the works, approaching the dugout with his pushcart, he almost ran over two officers.

"Steady, soldier!"

"Oh . . . "

"Is that how you greet an officer!"

"Sir . . . " said Richard.

Ralph appeared behind the officers, a captain and a colonel. The unit was not used to such brass in the tunnels.

"Private!" Ralph barked. "Move this gear aside so the C.O. can get through."

The C.O.!

The officers shuffled by, grumbling. Ralph watched them go.

Richard eased from attention when they rounded the curve.

"What's that all about?"

"Well you should ask, my boy, well you should ask."

Ralph seemed distracted. In a month of working together, Richard had not seen him this way.

"Get the smokes?"

"Sure."

"Good man."

Ralph took the package.

"Get the guys together. Bring 'em to my hole."

"Okay."

When the ten men of the unit were all in Ralph's office and the air was thick with tobacco smoke the sergeant casually rolled out a map and poked a finger at it. "We're here." He dragged a heavy stream through his cigarette and exhaled over the map. "Those peacocks you saw in here were the C.O. and his orderly. They want us to dig up to here . . . "

Ralph moved his finger along the map. "For those of you lacking in map-reading skills I'll make it simple for you. At this section we got about eight hundred yards between them and us. That's comfortable. That's 'cause it's quiet around here.

"Those clowns you saw leaving . . . " The sergeant looked around. Richard saw for the first time a sadness in his eyes that his jocular manner could not cover. "They want us to go from where we are to about mid-point. Four hundred more yards until we're at Heine's doorstep. They figure on heating things up.

"We're going to lay a mine right there. There's gonna be an attack. They're going to have the standard-type barrage and then we blow the mine and then they're going to attack. The bad part is that they want it in three weeks."

The men in the tunnel gasped.

"That's right."

"That's crazy," Richard said.

"There you go using logic, Richard. What did I say about that? Where does it get you?"

"We can't do it."

"They think we can."

The men grumbled.

Ralph took another long pull on his cigarette and flicked it to the ground. "It'll be tough but we're gonna do it right. No chances. Everybody keep safe. I'll be up there with you."

Exactly twenty days later—after the squad lost two men because of a cave-in and a further three from fatigue—the tunnel system stretched from the peaceful front lines Richard was so fond of traversing all the way to a dark and secret hole of approaching terror. It was filling rapidly with every bit of explosive headquarters could free up. In all, they packed six tons of TNT into the cramped space. Richard worked until the end, wishing he would collapse like the lucky ones, hauled away for rest and relieved by wide-eyed replacements.

The replacements especially depressed Richard. They looked like Charlie, just before he died. The secret to life here, he deduced, was getting that look out of your eyes. Feel the fear, okay, but don't look like you're coming apart or you surely will. That's the ticket. Keep your eyes open and your fear under control. And don't let anybody tell you anything under fire, keep to yourself.

The day of the attack, Sergeant Ralph had more bad news.

"They want us to stay up here for the detonation and then go to the observation posts to help the advance."

"How far up?"

"This far." Ralph pointed to the map.

"We'll die," said Richard.

"No we won't."

"That close it'll punch our eardrums in and make soup of our brains. I've seen what close explosions will do. It's crazy."

"There you go using logic again."

"It's not funny."

"I don't need you to tell me it's not funny, Private."

Ralph's shift of tone stiffened their backs. Richard knew enough to shut up.

"We'll survive this thing and follow orders. But it's gonna be ticklish. You gotta do as I say."

At zero minus thirty minutes, attack day, the squad was spread down through the tunnel well back from the explosives, sitting in several small dugouts fashioned specifically to dull the concussion of an underground explosion. Ralph had been careful to position the stations close enough to the front to satisfy headquarters that his men would be ready, after the detonation, to leap from their breathing holes and man forward observation posts for the advancing troops. At zero minus twenty, the captain appeared.

"Sergeant, your men are too far back."

"Sir, I've gone over the plan carefully. We'll be in position."

"Sergeant, the colonel has reviewed your plans and believes it imperative that you be no further than three hundred yards from the terminus at the time of detonation. He wants your men on top immediately afterward to transmit details of the damage. We must know if the wire is still standing, where the holes are."

"Sir, the men will die of concussion."

"We don't think so."

"Sir, maybe we should take up the surface post before the detonation."

"We can't risk a sighting. So far we have total surprise."

"Sir, this is unwise, with all respect . . . "

"Sergeant, do as you are asked, please."

Richard heard this conversation from his buried concealment a few yards away. He was the first one Ralph pointed to and motioned upward. The captain stayed in the tunnel long enough to see him emerge.

"Quickly," the captain said to his watch. "Zero minus fifteen."

"We'll die, Ralph."

"You don't know that for sure."

"Yes I do."

"No, you don't."

"Trust me."

"I do trust you, kid. But that won't help us, will it?"

"We gotta go up top."

"And risk a firing squad? I'd rather take my chances down here."

"It won't work."

"I know your opinion, Richard. Now do as we're told."

At zero minus three minutes, the underground squad lay along a fifty-yard stretch of the tunnel, covered with as much dirt as they dared, expecting much more to come down once the mine blew. Richard tried to block out the death signals going off in his brain. He could not. One of the exit spurs was directly to his right. With two minutes to go, the tunnel in darkness, he uncovered himself and crawled for the hole.

The plan came to him the instant he saw the cool blue sky outside the hole. Stay here for the explosion, you won't be seen, you've got a chance to survive the concussion. As another minute ticked by, Richard stuck his head out of the hole and took a full breath of fresh air.

Though he did not know the exact moment the mine went up, Richard was aware of a pressure and a punishing general blow that filled the world and resonated for a long time. The result of his position at the breathing vent and the force of the explosion was propulsion, magic trajectory which did not seem real while happening but in the remembering was spectacular and exhilarating.

As he tumbled feet first into a shell-crater, rolling over and over without his rifle, helmet and one of his boots, Richard was already marveling that a human could fly so far and high and still be alive. He'd seen the enemy lines, the wire, the rise of the massive detonation two football fields away. Like a map it had seemed, laid out logically. He'd seen again the grey dots, brandishing shiny bayonets. Then earth had rushed up to him and in the grace of it he felt he'd been able to choose his spot, a gentle slope of landing, in the soft tossed-soil basin of the crater.

Richard snapped from his reverie, shaking his head. What happened?

I flew in the air. No. It's a dream. A nightmare.

Yes, a nightmare.

As Richard sat in his hole that sound came again—the voices, a chorus of wails. Bombs and the tearing damage they were doing to breathing bodies. It killed him in his guts to hear it again and no less so this time that it was the other side screaming and running, bent for death. The shells that landed now with fury did not drown the sound.

The shells dropped. Richard looked around, sizing.

Yes, I can stay here.

Bullets hit the lip of the crater. Richard concentrated on their vibration through the ground to his fingertips. He followed their pattern, stops and starts.

Yes, I can stay here for the time being. And if I have to run it will be that way and then that way to that other crater and then that way to that ditch.

Richard concentrated his senses and hugged the ground. The wail died away but then there was another vibration, footsteps, and a soldier dropped into the hole with him.

"Christ, fella!" the man exclaimed, "I thought I was all alone out here."

"I been here for a while."

"You have! Where's your helmet and boot?"

Richard began to answer as a shell landed behind the man and he fell forward in the dirt, his back a bloody mass.

Fairly natural. You stand in the rain, you're going to get killed.

Richard picked up his rifle, checked the action and looked around. Others had made it to his position and were advancing slowly through the mayhem. Richard saw the route he could take to join them. Step here. Crouch. Yes. It's safe. Step. Step.

Many men were now marching through, crouched, stopping, starting, falling. Some were in craters, resting, stopping to hold wounds, catch breath. Richard walked easily, knowing where to step, scaring himself at times with the closeness of bullets and metal around him. He felt wind on his face from close-singing machine-gun slugs seeking him. He wanted to call out to the men beside him, occasionally getting a sense of the next danger, never getting through to them in the clamour as the shrapnel cut or the bullets punched them breathless and dead.

He kept on. As many as fell around him more were coming along. Richard felt a sad exhilaration at the willingness of all of them to be there to do this and try to see their way. It was an enormity of sadness, a choking fatal blanket. Richard gagged, knowing that if the bullets didn't get him, and he doubted they could, this emotion surely would. He choked, fought off the feeling. It was just like fear, a killer. It was wider, took longer to get you, but get you it would.

Richard began to run, careless. He felt himself getting

away from the choking. When he felt it lifting, still among falling bodies, he eased up, remembering.

No more holes.

The attack went badly. Headquarters never received communications from the front about the efficacy of the mine, and troop movement could not be visually observed because of the heavy bombardment. After twenty minutes the retreat was sounded.

Richard was far beyond the bugle call or the whistles and would not have heard anyway for the clatter of machine-gun fire that now filled his ears. Sitting carefully in a hollow among the torture-bristling concertina wire, he was below the sight lines and thus safe from the leaden river flowing ten inches above his head.

The more he listened though, the more he became hypnotized by the angry, violent noise. Somehow, being so close to this nasty animal and yet being so safe from it brought a hazy comfort he'd seldom known.

When the guns stopped the interruption was a wakening. Richard spied through the wire and thought he saw where the emplacement was—the scramble of activity around it—reloading, black-helmeted observers craning out across the death-strewn barbed wire coils.

Richard felt the rifle in his hands.

I've dodged death. How does it work the other way around?

He crawled a few yards to the side, trying not to disturb the wire. After a few minutes, he found a gap where a shell had landed and then he advanced far enough so he could see the area the mine had blown. The bomb had carved a gap in the enemy's trench-line, tossing up debris and pushing the wire forward but not breaking it. The mine had been set too far forward.

All that digging. All that death.

The machine-gun crew had perched themselves on the far side of the crater, out of the line of any fire but closely watching the front. Richard was far enough to the side not to be noticed. He brought the rifle to his cheek and settled into the ground.

Should I do this?

The machine-gun ammo loader had his back to him.

I can't shoot a guy in the back, 'specially the first time.

The gunner was at his sights, glaring into the battlefield, pinching off bursts wherever he sensed movement.

He's the killer. He's the dead.

Richard sighted for the man's head, noting that in the perfect line of barrel and target he was murderously close. As his finger developed pressure he knew there was no possibility he could miss. He felt near enough to almost touch the man. He squeezed the trigger.

The gunner sprang from his crouch and fell backward, splayed. The loader, dumbfounded, swung around, leaping for the trigger-grip and yarding the thick barrel to point in Richard's direction.

Richard shot again and tore the loader's throat away. From this range Richard saw too much of the result. The man lurched forward, standing straight, clutching at his erupting wound.

In the terrible spectacle Richard debated with himself whether or not it was a blessing the man had no voice-box left to scream with. Then he felt himself moving toward losing control. Like with fear, like with sadness, like a knife being pressed slowly, agonizingly into his chest, he knew he had to fight it.

Yelling and the sound of movement and machinery issued from beyond the machine-gun emplacement. Heads appeared, clad in steel. Richard tore his eyes away from the struggling soldier, now prone in the dirt kicking his feet in futile agony. More were coming, what to do?

Kill more?

Not now.

Richard felt chilled though he was warm enough and had been sweating. For the first time since crawling into enemy territory he felt alone. He shrunk through the gap in the wire as the voices grew strong and the machine-gun started up again, seeking him. He crawled, enjoying the closeness of the ground on his chest. The bullets wailed by his head. The sound of it all was deadly, the essence of fear, but the vibration the rifle had made in his hand, the sight of the deaths he'd made, banished any fear. The image of the doomed gunner would not leave his mind. He tried not to picture his own death in a similar way. The imagining of it was too horrible. It was so horrible Richard knew it would never happen to him. Rational or not, he knew it would never happen to him.

For two days Richard crawled around no-man's-land, making it in his mind no-man-but-Richard's-land and he caught himself often chuckling at the thought. He then began to fear only that he might go starkly mad, rave like a starving dog and attract attention from either side. But no one found him.

He located one of the breathing holes the squad had dug and thought of going in to see what had happened but knowing what he'd find he chose instead to become a crawling gypsy.

He took enough rations off corpses to keep going and

carefully avoided the recovery parties when they sortied to remove the dead. It wasn't time to go yet. There was something he had to do, a last liability to dispense with before going back and trying to survive the rest of this experience.

On the night of the second day he dropped down into an enemy trench. He'd watched this particular stretch all day, knew it was scarcely manned, could tell by sound and action what type of place it was. He crouched to the duckboards watching either direction for movement. He had heard the sentry pass minutes before, knew the man would be back in about thirty seconds, fixed his bayonet and waited in the shadows.

Because the battle was long over, the sector was now quiet again. The only artillery action was twenty miles away. In the lulls of quiet it was possible to hear a man's footfalls on the damp wood.

Then there were indeed footfalls, the sentry returning. Richard sensed there was no fear in the shadow he was now watching because it was so unlikely there would be anything to worry about. A recon squad would have strict orders not to come into intentional contact. The sector was quiet. There was no reason for any enemy action here. All these things reaffirmed for Richard the purity of what he was about to do.

Yes, senseless.

If this horror was going to go on, sanctioned by powers who could take somebody from the other side of the world and plunk them down on this pretty countryside to kill and be killed themselves in any number and variety of grotesque ways, then by the will of Richard it would go on at full volume, open throttle to the end. And thus end quicker. And the method would be savagery. Abject, animal, abominatory craziness.

The shadow stepped to within five feet of Richard. The bayonet smiled a flash on its way to the target but did not give sufficient warning for anything but fear to arrive. In the dark, Richard saw the man's eyes flare. He aimed the point toward fatal ribs and lunged, abandoned and sacredly powerful.

The victim dropped his weapon so as to grasp the shaft which pushed him backwards, stumbling into the wall of the trench. With no room left to retreat, the blade crushed through bone and began to enter the chest. The slowness of this murder allowed every bit of pain to dwell. The man screamed and shrieked, then gurgled benignly as the blade punctured a lung.

Richard pushed until he felt the blade exiting into the dirt wall behind. He pulled back abruptly, shocking the victim still further, the face disbelieving that he could be designed to feel this much pain. With the point somewhere in the man's chest, Richard began twisting and jimmying, making further disaster in the chest cavity. The victim shook at the end of the deadly stalk, hands grasping at air, arms flailing. Blood projected from his mouth, spouting so that Richard could not see his expression any longer.

The ritual went on until Richard was holding the dead man upright with great effort upon the end of his lance. He heard running footsteps, yanked the blade out with difficulty, the rasp of metal on rib-bone making a teeth-grating sound like fingernails down a blackboard.

Then Richard leapt to the parapet and was gone in darkness, scramble-crawling away through the wire.

An hour later his hands were still steady, his nerves superhuman calm. He had recognized a certain need and felt proud having attained it. The essence of the war was something he now knew, had experienced in his fingertips and saved in his bones. He felt he was a lethal machine, made for existence in this mud and terror.

Richard crawled toward Company Headquarters, where he knew he'd be greeted with indifference and peevish resentment at best. At worst a court martial. A straggler who needed reassigning or punishing. He did not care.

His hands did not shake. Though he knew that his revelation on the battlefield would carry him through this hell, he wondered if death in an instant, a bullet in the brain and a mass grave outside a town with a cathedral might not be so bad in the long run.

« 1916 »

Some of them, including Richard, walked from Belgium to France. There was a new salient, new commanders, some better equipment, but the same pitiful look in the eyes of replacements and the same enemy in the same war. It was bigger now. Richard was attached to an infantry company at one of the worst places in the line.

Arriving at the rear emplacements, not far from the boom-rumbling, air-sucking heavy artillery, Richard reported to his company. He hoped only to deal with the orderly sergeant, avoiding the glances of officers. Headquarters was in a small village.

The sergeant looked at Richard, then at the orders. His face was tight, lips closed, eyes darting. Richard sized him for a regular. Experienced.

"Been at Loos, have you, Private?" The sergeant's voice was surprisingly soft, almost warm. "Ypres too, I see. And Festubert and 'The Orchard'."

"Aye. All of those places, Sergeant."

Silence. The sergeant went to the door of a cottage and knocked gently. From inside a voice called: "Yes?"

"If you don't mind, sir."

"One moment."

The sergeant returned. "Did you see the gas?"

"Lots of times."

"Mostly at Second Ypres, I guess."

"Givenchy, too. And Messines . . . "

Richard was becoming uncomfortable. Not so much at having recollected those infamous days when without masks men had plunged their heads into the mud, breathed through urine-soaked rags or simply gone off their heads trying to escape the green gagging death-clouds. That wasn't so bad. What was so bad was having no place to hunker away from this open, standing invitation to death: an obvious headquarters in an exposed village. With every second villager a probable spy/observer for Fritz's gunnery. Richard treasured his gift, his commitment to no more punctures, but this was abusing it. The interview had better end soon.

The cottage door opened and Captain Jason Speckley strode through. His uniform shone its newness.

"Richard!"

"Hello . . . sir."

"Holy . . . You mean you've been fighting all this time and you haven't got killed or sent home for insulting officers or anything?"

"No, sir."

"And you respect officers now. Amazing."

Richard did not answer. The sergeant took his opportunity.

"You know this man, sir?"

"Know him. He saved my life. He's the one who actually earned these . . . " Jason pointed to the colourful line of ribbons on his tunic. "He grew up right beside me, used to play soccer on the field behind our house."

"I thought, owing to his experience, he might be a good raider, sir. I was about to assign him to the recon group, with your permission, sir."

"What do you feel like doing, Richard? It's up to you."

Richard allowed himself to look at Jason, in the eyes, for the first time. They were clear, with an honesty he found hard to confront. They bored right into him and he averted his gaze after a second. "Whatever you say," he said.

"Private!" The sergeant barked. "Address an officer with the proper respect."

"Yes, sir." Richard said.

Jason stepped closer and held out his hand. "Sergeant, assign Private Delta to the recon group. He'll make an excellent raider." He touched Richard on the arm. "Walk with me."

They strolled down the village street, dodging dispatch riders on growling motorcycles.

"There's big stuff going on. Glad I got out of the hospital in time."

"You should have gone home."

"And leave you to all this glory? Never. Besides, the brass started using me for publicity. More pictures in the English papers than the King."

"You should have stayed over there. It's no good for guys like you over here."

"What do you mean by that? I got a glory wound. I have you to save my life again."

"I'm not saving anybody's life but mine."

The tone of Richard's voice put silence between them for a few moments.

"How come you're still a private?"

"Why not?"

"You're a veteran. Been through more stuff than the average general."

"The average general doesn't want to know that."

Jason shrugged, looking at Richard with resigned sadness. "Still the little outlaw."

"That's a funny word to use out here."

"You should stop trying to fight yourself, old friend. People could do you favours. I could do you favours. You deserve it . . . "

"That's all right."

"No it's not. You're a special man. I want to see you come out of this. I'll never forget what you did . . . "

"I didn't do anything. You acted like a fool and I went along with you. Don't expect me to do it again."

For a second time the vehemence of Richard's words and his voice brought silence down. Jason stopped walking and turned, looking up the narrow street. "I have to go. I'll come see you."

"Fine."

"Good to see you again, Richard."

"Fine," Richard said.

The reconnaissance gang had ten men permanently

assigned. With one glance Richard saw that three were killers, like him. The others would be gone too soon to care about. The sergeant was not one of the killers, not worth listening to. Richard and the hard men stood off while the non-com addressed the squad.

"Men, there's orders coming down this evening and we're pretty sure there's something up. There's never been such a big army assembled anywhere on the face of this earth. You're a part of history, all of ya. Right where you stand."

Richard turned away, sickened. A year now he'd spent, walking and crawling through this business and he'd heard this speech many times. Every time the words came from a dead man. And those who listened—they were dead too.

"We're gonna be the pointy end of an attack. A big attack. If all goes well this'll put an end to it. Home by Christmas, boys."

Richard had heard these 'Home-by-Christmas-Easter-Thanksgiving' speeches where the men actually cheered. Now, at least, they just kept their heads down and looked at one another, trying not to hope too much. He looked over at the killers; he thought he saw a mirthful smile on one of them.

Fine.

The one saving grace was that it was summer. Crawling on your gut you didn't get so muddy and there was a chance of sleeping dry most of the time. On the other hand, lying out for days on your belly, dust grinding on your teeth, you went through copious quantities of water and had to arrange for drops to exchange canteens. This caused the dangerous necessity of pre-arranged meetings, bunching up bodies and providing that much more chance of being spotted and summarily pounded with mortars or pinged with machine-guns or hunted by raiding parties or combinations of all three.

That July, Richard and his comrades operated for a continuous two-week period, from the beginning of the Somme offensive until the mistaken, insane carnage took a lull before blazing on for a further three months of incompetent human wastage. During that time the non-killer segment of the squad was lost quickly and the frenetic times disallowed headquarters sending another sergeant to replace the one who'd had his brains blown out trying to cut wire near a pillbox. The action had been ill-conceived from the start but unlike times before Richard had not attempted to dissuade or advise. He'd learned it was useless.

Now there was only Frank, Simon and himself. Bill, the other professional, had caught a mortar shard in the thigh and hauled himself off to the rear, over the stacked bodies of their comrades rotting in the sun since the morning of the first attack. The three repaired back to a forward trench, formerly of the enemy, to replenish canteens and try to find out what was happening.

Richard was almost finished filling his two canteens, stuffing biscuits in his pockets and scrounging some trench bombs when someone down the line snapped to attention and saluted. An officer came from an underground passage, sweeping the burlap aside and striding confidently into the trench.

Richard saw that it was Jason Speckley only after it was too late to flee.

"You shouldn't come here." Richard spoke without introduction. "Stay back with headquarters."

"Orders, chum." Captain Speckley gestured to the meagre squad. "I have to go with you and your friends."

"You can't."

"You're forgetting yourself again."

Richard remembered the futility of argument. His mind hardened, visualized this man's death. Who was he, anyway? The familiarity of a man from his home town no longer held value to him. Speckley came from a time and place that had no relation to now.

Fine. You want to die, be my guest.

"You have to observe?" Richard asked.

"Artillery accuracy, wire cutting efficacy, casualties . . . "

"Plenty of those. Why don't they send a non-com, or lieutenant if they have to have an officer . . . "

"None left. If you know what I mean."

Richard looked again, for a fleeting moment, into Jason's eyes. Sadness. Concern. No murder, though.

"Stick close to me. We'll take it slow."

"Don't worry about me."

Richard did not answer. Nor did he indicate verbally to the others that it was time to depart. No one was in charge. The men took less notice of Captain Speckley than they would a fellow private. There was silent professionalism in the air, each man personally prepared. They mounted the ramparts and crawled under a lumber gun-emplacement, through an earthen tunnel and into the cluttered moonscape of the battlefield.

No words were spoken. The four crawled, spread over fifty yards of territory, progressing unevenly through the wreckage of a battle that had begun in heat and great sacrifice but now continued in drudgery and pain. The bodies of the first day's slaughter were decomposing in the sunlight, faces impossibly black, like pictures of Africans in schoolbooks. Richard was aware of Jason's distress at seeing and smelling the first of the many large groups of heaped corpses. He heard the gagging, then retching. He stopped, annoyed but aware that the sooner Jason's mission was completed the sooner Richard could be alone again in this familiar hell.

They moved forward. A shell landed nearby, close enough to send dust their way and colour everything tan. Jason rolled closer to Richard and whispered: "Have they seen us?"

"Not likely. That was ours."

"Ours?"

Another shell came over, this time breaking further ahead of them, closer to the enemy lines. The direction of the vibration as it approached, the particular sound of the British-built ordinance, told Richard that their own artillery was active.

Jason was mouthing something that could not be heard. Now that they'd found the range the artillery was sending over a hail of explosives. Richard turned to the officer and held his mouth to his ear.

"This is what you wanted to see, isn't it?"

"I didn't know it would be so close!"

"Close?" The explosive rain was approaching total saturation and talk became useless as neither man could hear anything but the auditory-overload buzz of their eardrums being damaged.

Close? We're not even near close!

It was Jason's fearful look that set Richard's thinly-controlled anger off.

"Close!" He screamed it to himself. "Close! I'll show you close!"

Richard grabbed Jason's sleeve and pointed toward where the explosions had sent up a dirt curtain, blocking the sun, making it eerily amber-dark. Richard stood up and snatched Jason to his feet. The officer reluctantly stood, hunched over.

"Come on," Richard screamed, darting off across the terrain in a weaving, hopping pattern, light on his feet like a ballet dancer. Jason followed, noticing on either side the other men rising and running along with them, apparently confident that the artillery screen was protection enough.

They came to a depression, wide and long, and Richard flung Jason to the ground. They were at the base of the enemy ramparts, the slow rise steepening toward a broad parapet.

A sound beyond the barrage came to them. Machine-gun. Richard pulled a trench bomb from his pack. With a darting look at Jason that said, "Follow me," he leapt toward the top of the trench and hurled the bomb up and to the side.

At the small explosion, barely heard above the close-by crashing of artillery, Richard swept up the rise and motioned for Jason to follow him overtop, then disappeared. The officer scrambled behind him, wielding his pistol.

Richard stood over two bodies. He waited for Jason to clear the top of the trench before firing a shot point-blank into the face of one of the prone men. A snap of the bolt and another bullet smashed the face of the other. Richard could see that his offhand manner of savagery shocked Jason so much he almost dropped his pistol. The others appeared at the lip of the trench, tumbled down, rifles at the ready, and fanned along either side of the trench.

There were wounded lying here and there, damaged by the barrage, which was now walking its giant way further to the rear. Richard, Simon and Frank began systematically dispatching the immobilized with bullet and bayonet. Jason stood by and avoided watching, but shot a man who leapt at Richard from a dugout. Though he had anticipated the surprise and had had his bayonet ready, Richard was impressed at the way Jason's instinct had taken over, raising the pistol automatically and pulling the trigger before any decision good or bad, one way or another could be made. The gunned soldier dropped to his knees, blood at the mouth. He fell forward into the dirt, sending up a puff of dust. A gaping wound glistened high up in the centre of his back. Jason fidgeted with his pistol.

Richard strode past the fresh corpse, gripped Jason's arm and pulled him to follow. The others came behind. The barrage had moved far back by now. The party swept quickly up the trench, rounded a bend. Richard raised his hand. Frank and Simon fell immediately against the side of the trench, grabbing Jason down with them.

A column of grey-clad men, six in all, filed in as if connected to a communication trench twenty yards ahead. Richard and Simon and Frank were shooting profusely before the last of the column was fully exposed. Richard whipped his prized captured Luger from the front of his tunic and blasted away, calmly taking aim, making each shot count. Jason raised his weapon and fired once.

The column died in seconds, each man given a *coup de gras* by the killing team before they moved further down the trench. Jason stumbled along with them. Richard imagined he was too shocked by the general indecency of it all to ask himself where they might be going.

Walking, scouting, reloading at the same time, Richard was in a far-off land where there existed no deviation from the central rule: If you're not with me you're dead. No exceptions. That's the order from hell. The only order that counts.

Richard again raised his hand. The others tensed, looking the situation over, wordless, then took positions on either side of the dugout entrance Richard had located. It was a bigger affair than they'd seen earlier, denoting greater importance. Richard undid his last trench bomb and slipped it inside the curtain.

Seconds later the curtain blew off into the trench, dust erupted from the entrance and Simon stepped to the gaping hole and hurled another bomb violently down the passage. Again there was a blowing of dust, though not so vigorously as the bomb had penetrated deeper into the hole, perhaps getting around one or two of the turns dug into the entrance to mitigate against such attack. Leveling his rifle with one hand, pistol in the other, Richard stepped into the entrance, downward into the dugout. Simon followed two paces behind. In a few moments Richard gestured to him to collect the other men inside. A few grey forms lay about, covered with dust. Richard, pistol in hand, found a leather case on a crude table in the middle of the room.

He turned to Jason. "This any good to you?"

Richard fingered documents, a map.

Jason moved to the table and peered at the material in the scant light of one candle still burning in its bracket on a wall. Maps, several documents with much script, a few dispatch forms, some small cloth-bound booklets.

"Treasure," Jason managed to say.

"Grab it, then . . . "

Richard hastily wrapped the bundle back into the pouch and thrust it at Jason.

A groan came from the floor in one corner. The three assassins swung toward the sound, guns at the ready.

A hand rose from the dirt and wiped at a face. The shiny bars of officer rank stood out from the grey cloth of the sleeve. Richard drew a careful bead with his Luger.

"Don't! It's an officer, a prisoner."

Richard looked at Jason blankly.

"What?"

"We're taking him back."

"We're too far out on a limb," Richard said. "Just kill him."

"No. We've come this far. Let's try it."

"You've got your stuff. You're a hero again. Don't push it."

"Richard," Simon said, "we're movin'."

"Right."

A sound had come from outside. Frank and Simon went to a passage at the back of the dugout.

"We gotta go. He dies . . . " With the last word, Richard squeezed the trigger. He had been looking at Jason but the gun never left the face of the wakening victim. Blood splashed as high as the candle on the wall.

Jason stepped backward, shocked and stumbling. "You'll follow orders one day," he uttered. "I swear."

"Orders. Can orders save you in here?"

Richard made for the tunnel Frank and Simon had gone down, leaving Jason alone, clutching his bundle of documents. He could already hear harsh voices at the smashed entrance-way and he knew Jason would make for the back tunnel and run as fast as the darkness would let him. Still, he listened for the officer's progress behind him.

Richard had developed a talent for knowing when the appropriate tool was most indicated: rifle, pistol or bayonet. On the run back through the tunnel system, the foursome burst into the light directly in front of a field kitchen. Luckily, no troops were present, but the cooks had time to grab knives, pistols and clubs. The three killers fought efficiently amid the knowledge that one slip—a badly aimed shot, a clumsy thrust of blade—and the whole fabric would tear. They'd all die. But the trio had perfected an artful blood-ballet; Richard worked surgically, ducking, firing, dodging and dispatching seven men in under twenty seconds.

The firefight over, Frank grabbed bread and sausage off one of the tables and the group ran along a trench. Then along toward the front, the enemy front, and over the last trench, crawling on their bellies trying not to be seen by either side. When they felt certain no one would notice them they flopped into their six-inch nether-world, relaxing in that lower skim of no-man's-land that they then proved was indeed some-men's-land.

Huddled in a crater at sundown, they ate.

"Richard, I've got to get back with these documents."

"Be my guest, Captain."

"You or one of your men should escort me."

"Nobody is my man, Captain."

"Then you come, I'm . . . "

"Ordering me . .?"

"Yes."

Frank and Simon laughed, chewing on bread and sausage.

"Tell you what," Richard said, trying not to be too disrespectful and failing. "we're refusing that order, so you crawl back there and send some MPs to come and get us."

The men laughed harder.

Jason moved to the rear of the shell-hole. He turned back to Richard. "Someday you'll feel differently about the civilized world."

"Good-bye, Cap."

Hugging his captured papers, Captain Jason Speckley crawled away into the blood-dusted gloom.

« 1917 »

Richard lost his two most efficient confrères in the chill of the October death, the end of the Somme disaster and lull before the other catastrophes that would occur before men stopped dying in the French mud. They'd gone out with pneumonia.

Richard did not know what kept him alive through the cold, because he could feel it in every cell of his body. He coughed deeply and rough. The skin of his feet was coming off with his socks. It was a fortunate month when he got a change of clothes. The time now did not seem to pass. It just hung. It felt a blank eternity since he'd come to the war. He could barely remember a childhood and didn't try. He'd always been a soldier. He'd always be a killer. He did not think of what he might do or what he might be afterward. Aside from killing and surviving, Richard did not think.

The harshness of winter stopped much of the war machinery along the front in France. But early spring brought renewed resolve on the part of the armies to exercise, to justify their existences in this muddy district. Richard was called to headquarters by a reluctant sergeant, a man who knew the sullen lad with the hidden Luger who preferred the dangerous solitude of the dying fields to the reassuring camaraderie of the dugouts. The sergeant did not know why headquarters would want to speak specifically to any private, let alone this one.

To Richard, it could only mean one thing. Jason Speckley, with his bundle of enemy documents, had made it back that night nine months ago.

Richard was ushered into a headquarters cottage. Jason, with major's pips on his shoulder, looked up from a desk.

"That will be all, Sergeant. Please leave us."

"Very good, sir."

The sergeant left, closing the door heavily.

"How've you been, Richard?"

"Cold."

"I know. Our casualties have been heavy with it . . . "

The silence between them then was leaden as wet wool. Richard did not wish to expend resources to relieve it.

He wants to talk, let him make the conversation. Meanwhile, here I am again in a headquarters building, being sized up for a peasant's coffin just as soon as anybody can get word to a good gunnery hand about where the so-called brains are on the other side.

"It seems," Jason said, "that the kind of war you want to fight is coming into fashion."

The statement hung for a while.

"You're the kind of man, Richard, that we don't know what to do with. You buck orders, respect no one. You're a complete law unto yourself. You avoid contact with officers, non-coms and most other men. You don't even take your leaves, for heaven's sake. Some people like you desert. That's logical. But you desert toward the enemy. You're most comfortable where you're least likely to survive. Because it keeps you away from people like me, I suppose."

Richard, having thought all this out and then forgotten it almost two years and many lifetimes ago, had no response.

"I'd like to offer you a field promotion to the rank of sergeant. I need you to use your special . . . skills."

"I don't think it'll work."

"It doesn't matter what you think."

"We're back to that again."

"Look, don't you have any feeling for those fellows out there? You think they want to be live targets any more than you do? You've got talent. It seems to only work for you, but, if we can get some of it to rub off . . . "

"Don't blame me for the war. Don't blame me for learning how to fight it . . . this is stupid."

"Listen to me and shut your mouth. In two weeks we're moving up somewhere around Arras. Another hot sector. There's this ridge, the English and French have lost a lot of men on it. It's an observation point for Fritz. We've got to get him out of there. High Command is impressed with our—your work here."

"It's all the same to me. Let's go."

"I want you to build a special unit."

"They'll all die as soon as we get into the field."

"What about those two that were with us last summer?"

"Both gone. Pneumonia."

"There has to be others."

"Sure there are. But you won't find them. Neither will I.

They're out there. As far away from here as possible."

"There's got to be some way of organizing them. Think of what they could do under a central command."

"You don't understand. There is no central command."

"There must be. How could all this be going on without one?"

A pause.

"Exactly," said Richard, sighing.

The Battle of Vimy Ridge took a week of slogging through mud and snow, attacking frontally a line of fortified defenses. Thirty-five hundred men fell during that week and didn't get up. There was talk of certain lone soldiers who appeared during particularly hard times, charging machine-gun emplacements, throwing bombs into pillboxes. Many decorations were won by corpses lying about smoking ruins.

Richard saw the battle in all its phases, and played his assassination instrument stridently amid the general discordant murder.

Because of the difficulty of positive identification, the disorganization of the armies, the infancy of field telecommunications, the plethora of bodies sliced everywhere and the creeping, general loss of belief among the soldiers, much of Richard's work is lost to history. But an important part of his life proclaimed itself one moment when he came closest to death on his long march in the gothic darkness of a musty-lighted morning raid.

The mud was a sucking monster, accounting for many of the anonymous missing. Sometimes though, the mud was a friend because the shells would sink deep before exploding, sending a benign spurt of steamy spume upward and shaking the ground but leaving no one seriously hurt. The rumble of the subterranean explosions was something one felt in the fibres of the bone.

Richard accepted the death-tremors and as always decoded them for their direction and intent, interpreting each new series of artillery patterns for their likelihood of approach, then dodging and diving when necessary. Running, with machine-gun bullets pinging off helmets, singing in the air, pock-marking the muck, splashing laughing in the puddles, he sensed the approach of a cluster of shells, the giant pace pounding coming urgent by volume and importance in his inner ears and survival balance. He hopped over a crater ridge and somersaulted to stillness, estimating the rate of pace to be off slightly to the left rear, allowing the oncoming explosion plumes to proceed with calming confidence. That he was wrong was the most disconcerting of the elements of this important day, that he could possibly not be absolutely capable.

The explosion was to the left rear, but in degree much shorter in both ranges than Richard estimated. The eruption tore the ground a-fly by his feet and raised his prone being upward in a tumbling war-version of a circus trick, floating again in the weightless space. The impact, several yards onward and back-first into the soft-firm cradle of Mother's soil propelled the air in his lungs hissing outward, up into the moiling atmosphere of the battle.

Calm, he did not fight but let his heart even its beating, his lungs enlarge deliberately, ignoring the pain and shock. His brain vibrated annoyed against its casing. He tried to minimize as best he could the mistake and its long-term implications. He ended by relaxing in this temporary recess and gazing upward to the smoke-smudged grey sky and immediately considered the absurd image of a bird fluttering amidst the concert of hurtling lead.

In fact, a pigeon. Struggling too much, Richard saw, even with the turbulence of the air and the distractions of noise and smoke. He noticed then the awkward dangling paper, a leaf from an officer's dispatch book probably, waving and shifting weight, complicating flight procedure for the wrestling bird in an impossible feat of communication across the battlefield.

"Hah!" Richard had not intended to speak or make a sound. He had at this point not spoken for some twelve days, having avoided as was his expertise other humans for almost as long. But there it was, a sound acknowledging the desperate survivor straining overhead. He watched the bird circle, then make halting up-and-down progress toward the rear. The bullet wizz and zing was heavy, more than usual, and Richard's scarred consciousness miss-stepped then into emotional terrain where as yet he had not deigned to go. The bird jolted and dipped, hit slightly, lost feathers and spiraled toward the mud. At the final instant the brave thing recovered, labouring back to height and flying true as this crazy predicament would allow.

Richard hoped the water on his face was from a mud puddle, but then the heat of it, its magic origins within his face, pushed him beyond toughness and the denial of hope and he cried and cried as if born and raised to it, draining his tears to the cold October French soil, adding his feeling to all the other odd nutrients this ground would cull for its sustenance on into history.

The message pigeon flew struggling away, valiant. Richard rolled to his side, wiping and composing back to the machine-rolling killer he had chosen to become and proceeded on, forever then aware.

« 1926 »

One day when the drinking was at its worst he drove his car down a hill in New Westminster and crushed the skull of a seven-year-old girl playing with her dog by the side of the road.

He wondered why the dog was barking at him.

Later in his cell he had nightmares about a crying baby.

As his sentence wore on, the baby became older, the crying more strident and pitiful.

By the time the crying was of a plaintive seven-year-old, Richard had been admitted to a locked ward at Essondale. He was considered a bad case, mainly because of the danger the staff experienced in attending to his daily needs.

One rippling orderly who prided himself on being an expert in these kind of things took a deadly kick in the groin, suffering a ruptured scrotum.

After this incident Richard was judged untreatable and permanently shackled in a padded cell.

Still the wailing of a child haunted him and the terror of it and the stress further lowered his resistance and dignity.

His voice wore out from begging for death.

The nurses found it odd the way he cried for it:

"Puncture. Do me a hole, now . . . "

A nurse named Vivian, nineteen and straight out of school,

looked in on Richard one day. He'd been rolling around. It was morning and he was exhausted. He looked at her with frozen eyes, a brown stripe of smeared excrement across his mouth.

Vivian recoiled, gagging. Then she made herself look again.

This doesn't have to be so bad, she thought.

« 1956 »

The Oldsmobile Ninety-Eight was a bruiser of a car. Heavy, curved, confident. Richard was proud of the way he looked in it. It was a successful car for a successful man.

Not that a guy would need one of these things to define himself or anything like that. Not like the young kids with their cut-down, jacked-up, over-powered jalopies. Flame decals shooting out along the sides. Ridiculous. A good laugh. Some of the boys working for him, they had those kind of cars. Good kids. Seemed to need an outlet. Spent a hell of a lot of cash on these heaps. Let 'em. They were fine lads who worked hard. They worked hard to make Richard a successful man, one of the top building contractors in the city.

Richard drove his Oldsmobile Ninety-eight up Kingsway, taking a good lot of time to get to one of his projects. His last, maybe. Yes, maybe time to call it. Plenty of cash everywhere, the kids were all set up and gone. Time to give it a rest. That's what they told him. Everybody. They said: "Richard, you've worked hard. Time to ease up and enjoy a retirement. Especially now."

Especially now.

Richard pulled to the curb and gazed at the half-finished building, a three-storey low-rise with sixty units. Good, solid construction. Last at least a hundred years if somebody takes care of it.

It being Sunday, the site was deserted. Richard turned the ignition off and let the powerful car rumble down to silence. There wasn't much traffic. The peace and quiet penetrated him with an unexpected calm. Almost a contentment. Not a full contentment. Never all the way. Especially now.

If this is my last building . . .

Richard stepped from the car, selected keys and opened the swinging wire gate.

The building was fully framed and roofed. The doors and windows weren't in yet but some of the suites had been lathed and plastered. Richard roamed slowly, looking closely at joints, checking the quality of the work his boys were doing for him. It was there, the quality, right up to scratch.

My last building. A good one.

Richard climbed a near-completed stairwell to the top floor. The hallway was strewn with construction leavings, two-by-four ends, nail boxes and other trash. The place should have been cleared by now, at this stage. He went through the muck carefully to a suite, one of the large penthouse-style layouts they were building for the top-end crowd.

Maybe I should live in a place like this.

Richard strolled the skeletal rooms and paused at the

space left for the big picture window in what would be the living room. There was a spectacular view of the mountains. If you stood on tip-toe you could almost see the water.

The grandchildren could come and see, you could hold them up and they could see.

Several uneven pieces of left-over lumber were stacked against the back wall. Richard sat down on them, adjusted himself for comfort and considered the view. It was a beautiful day. The leaves were now fully out on the trees, muffling what traffic sounds there were. Richard felt like dozing and let himself drop off.

The dream was the one with the armoured car lurching south in the mud toward Amiens. In life Richard leapt from a water-filled ditch and strangled the officer as he leaned out the rear hatch, observing troop movements through his telescope. The gurgling was soft and did not alert the driver. Richard pulled his knife and crept through the vehicle. The plan was simply to cut a throat but as he approached Richard's scavenged peasant coat caught a corner of something and tore. The driver began to turn. Richard grabbed his shoulder and plunged the blade deeply upward into the chest, cutting sideways into the heart. A blast of blood heated his hand.

In the dream, as he whirled the man to face him, Richard saw that the man was actually a woman, barely a girl. She was Vivian.

Sleeping lightly, on the edge of consciousness, Richard fought for calm. His dream-training, painstakingly taught by the closest loved one he'd ever had, took over. Did he plunge the knife? He could not be sure. Was he doing it or thinking it? Vivian touched his face below his lower lip. He dropped the knife.

The blade hit the metal floor. The clatter woke Richard in mid-palpitation, gasping. He had fallen onto his side. It felt numb and made it awkward to regain himself. He struggled, wondering how much his aging heart could take of this recurrent nonsense. This uncontrollable annoying terrifying and crazy-making nonsense. He fought to remember the now, to live without memories if for only a few seconds so that he could stand straight and let the deathly throbbing of his heart ease off. He tried but could barely.

Vivian. Wiping his face.

He cursed, angry. He began to massage life back into his tingling leg. Gradually he felt better. He allowed thoughts of his late wife to proceed from his mind back into his heart.

That was her, still taking care of him in his dreams.

Dead a full year now and she was still his saviour.

You really should take a holiday. Retire, they said. Especially now.

A breath of coolish air struck him from the window. A cloud had blown across the view and the breeze stiffened to a wind, chilling him, making the half-built building feel like a refrigerator. Richard had a heady yearning for sunlight. He lurched into the cluttered hallway.

Stepping clumsy for the stairs, Richard stepped on a bent nail with such force that it penetrated the good-quality leather sole of his shoe and sent a cruel pain into his leg.

Howling, he hobbled down the stairs, out into the un-landscaped grounds and across to the car.

Sitting in the Oldsmobile, Richard laboriously extracted the nail with a pliers he kept in the glove compartment. The pain subsided. A tiny dot of red winked at him from the end of the nail.

He took the turn down Sperling and swung off toward the cemetery.

Walking back an hour later, still not warm enough though the sun shone brightly, Richard opened the car door and climbed in. His foot no longer hurt but his hands were shaking. He gripped the steering wheel with both hands.

He gripped harder.

Something didn't feel right. For the first time in the twenty-eight years since his resurrection something didn't feel right. It wasn't just the lack of Vivian. She had given him strength he didn't know he had. But it was his strength.

He took his hands from the steering wheel. What was happening?

He didn't feel strong anymore.

« 1982 »

If you take the MacDonald bus from Burrard you get a good connection to the westbound lines that go to Point Grey and the University of British Columbia. From downtown to home, no problem. Richard knew this. But now with the idea of going up Oak to the hospital the connections got all screwed up.

Mostly he didn't know what he'd do about a bathroom. Macdonald and Fourth there was the Chevron garage that didn't lock its doors. He worked it out perfectly. He could last until then, get off, do his business and take the #4 UBC up to Blanca and then walk the block-and-a-half back to his apartment with no problems.

No old man problems, pissing in your pants, squeezing out a fart and hoping it's just air and not the other.

But now with this going up to the hospital. What now?

Richard didn't know. Twice he'd tried it but couldn't make it. Might be time to wear one of those forsaken special underwear.

The thought of it made him quake.

There's gotta be a spot I can use!

Richard wondered if he could find the map his daughter had brought him a few years ago. The bedroom closet? Might be.

He spent an afternoon dismantling his bedroom closet. When the Meals-On-Wheels lady came she shrieked, scaring him.

"Mr. Delta! What have you done?"

"What have I done? Can't you see I'm looking for a map."

"A map?"

"You heard me. What am I having today? More paper beef?"

"You've made a big mess!"

"How 'bout some real steak for a change? I still got teeth, y'know . . . "

The Meals-On-Wheels lady went away and the next day a man came and put the closet back together. He handed Richard a new map of the city.

"It's got the transit routes right on it, Mr. Delta. See these red lines?"

"Huh?"

The hospital was big, a bigger place than Richard ever wanted to hang around. Too many people going too many places at once.

The lady at the desk looked up at him. "Yes?"

"I'm lookin' for a friend of mine. Jason Speckley."

The woman tapped at a computer keyboard.

"Are you sure he's in the hospital?"

"Sure I'm sure. He's here all right."

"Do you know what treatment he's having?"

"Treatment? Why, whatever it is you do around here. Treatment?"

"What is his medical difficulty?"

"Why, his difficulty is getting old. Like my difficulty. Like everybody's difficulty . . . "

"Hmmm . . . " She tapped again at the keyboard. "That's S-P-E-C-K-L-E-Y? With an E-Y?"

"Uh, that's right. I guess. How's that again?"

"He's in our long term care unit."

"And where might that be?"

"Back out the front entrance and around the side."

Richard was uneasy sitting in the chair looking out Jason's tiny window on the courtyard. He could see dozens of other tiny windows and knew there were hundreds more in this complex and many others like it. And behind each one a solitary staring old folk like this one—Jason—in a wheelchair holding a coffee mug with tea in it shaking to his lips.

"So they're keepin' ya, are they?"

Richard was surprised at Jason's sad smile.

"Nobody keeps anybody here, chum. They take you if there's room. You stay if you have to. And damn grateful . . . "

Richard scoffed, drank his tea.

"Get accustomed," Jason said. "God knows you've got more friends in than out of these places now, eh?"

"I'll not be coming here, myself."

"Hah! What spirit! Old toughie. How do you manage these days, anyhow? Waterworks still a bug?"

"I make out. Better than you here."

"Don't judge now."

"I'm not judging. It's just a helluva thing. Away from things as you are. Do you not miss your own spot?"

"Well I would like to go to the park . . . "

"Aye, the park."

"I would like to go sometime."

"Well, up with you. Let's trundle down now while the afternoon's good."

"Oh this is a little too soon for it."

"There's no too soon for two duffers standin' before ninety. There's no too soon for any at that age except death 'erself."

Jason smiled again. "And maybe not even that."

Richard looked at the floor. "Talk like that and I'll go myself. Leave you here to drool yourself dry waiting for them to feed you through a straw."

"Oh you're an irascible old toughie today."

"You've got me sittin' where I don't feel well put."

"Then there's nothing but to get a move on, I guess."

Jason stirred under his blanket. Richard took his tea mug and helped him from the chair.

They paused at the hospital entrance long enough for Richard to use the men's room. When he emerged a white-smocked woman was standing by Jason. She turned to Richard as he approached.

"You'll be careful now, won't you."

"Careful at what? We're two grown men going for a stroll. Who are you?"

"I'm the dietitian. I hope you'll have Mr. Speckley back for his evening meal."

"I should think that would be the prerogative of Mr. Speckley."

"Mr. Speckley is occasionally confused. Are you his friend?"

"You might say that. And I would heartily agree with you on the first comment. A man'd have to be mightily confused to check himself into a dungeon like this. And when he's still got legs enough to get to the park and back."

Jason chuckled at this. The woman smiled patiently.

"You gentlemen had better be on your way."

Richard helped Jason to his feet and they progressed to the street.

The Oak Street bus goes all the way down past the Veteran's long term care facility to downtown and beyond. Richard had checked it out. He and Jason climbed aboard, showed their pharmacare cards and because there was no room left at the front courtesy seats had to struggle down the crowded aisle to the back. Before they could get seated the bus lurched ahead, throwing Jason headlong into a young man in a business suit. Luckily the fellow was alert and before the bus moved was already in position to catch one or both of the unsteady old-timers. Richard had time to grip an overhead bar.

"Whoa," said the young man, easing Jason into a seat.

"I thank you," said Jason.

"Cursed abusers," muttered Richard, slumping into the seat beside Jason.

"Funny way of putting it," the young man chirped. "But I think I know what you mean." He returned to his newspaper.

Across from Richard and Jason a foursome of white-shirt-and-blazered private school boys spoke loudly among themselves.

"Yeah," said one, "the guy is like super nerd, y'know. Like he's right fucked all over. I don't know why he's even here."

"Aw fuck," said another, "he's just a fuckin' wimp-eyed klutzberg score. Afraid of his fuckin' shadow, like."

"Why doesn't somebody piss on his head or something?"

"Cause he'd fuckin' tell, right. Like he'd run all over raising shit like with the principal and everything. It's happened like about a hundred times."

"We should just drag him out of the sack some night and just pile shit on his head and scare the fuck out of 'um."

"I wanna get a baseball bat or something and smash his legs or something and kick his head in."

"Yeah kick his head in and stuff it with shit or something and make him real scared so his mom would have to come and get him."

"No, let's fuck his mom and hang her over his bed in the dark and scare the shit out of him that way."

"He's got too much shit in him."

Maniacal laughter.

Richard had had too much. "You boys, in the name of decency shut yourselves down there."

The boys paid no attention. The young man with the paper got up for his stop.

The boys continued.

"So what else do we do to him?"

"We take him out and cut his dink off and stuff it in his mouth, like. And kick the shit out of him and dump him on the steps or something."

"So everybody'd see."

"Yeah everybody'd see what a shitpile he was."

"Like I hate this guy, right."

"Oh like you're so different, like."

"No like I really hate this guy. He stinks like shit all the time, right."

The bus sped over the Cambie Bridge. Richard could not stand the sound of the boys. Jason seemed to be dozing. Others on the bus were doing their best to ignore the obscenity and disruption. Richard could not.

"Let's tie his sheets together and suffocate him in the dark so he doesn't see who's doing it."

"Let's wear hoods or something so he really freaks out."

"Naw, that might freak him out too much."

"Who fuckin' cares? I hate this guy."

Robson Street was full of people, as usual. Richard hoped the boys were getting off by the theatres, or the cluster of fast-food places, but they stayed on, prattling as loudly as ever their verbal violence. The bus continued slowly in thick traffic. Richard tried to screen the boys' voices from his consciousness.

"Like who let this guy live, anyway? He stinks like shit and eats his own snot, like. He's workin' for a kick in the balls with army boots on."

Richard tried his last. Anger blood-flowed acidly through him. Though he had forsaken violence sixty years past and forgotten it with a glorious recovery to the world the taste in his mouth was familiar. So was the tension in his muscles. He forgot about being eighty-four years old.

He rose to a steady planting upon his feet in the lurching bus and with a one-hand movement precise and unstoppable gripped the nearest boy in a vice-hold at the throat. The boys buzzed silent.

A woman stood and exclaimed something Richard did not hear.

The bus slowed and pulled over. Richard, lethal-steady, clasped another hand around the reddening boy's throat, lifting.

The driver approached. The whole bus was now quiet but for the gasping of Richard's victim. The other boys stared, saucer-eyed.

The driver touched Richard's wrist. Felt the steel of it. He looked at the old man's face and saw the killer. It rendered him cold, unable to think. "What are you going to do, sir?" he finally asked.

Richard did not speak or move. He was away. Fighting. But then there was a turmoil rising in his chest, an ill-feeling like never before. It traveled to his head and down his arms. As it closed on his hands Richard let the boy slowly go, his fingers losing their power. Though the will, unfaded, to squeeze the boy's life away—crush the voice box, feel the bony collapse of the wind-pipe in his hands—was still there. God help him, Richard knew he had not the strength and was elated almost to crying out.

Thank God, Vivian.

The driver pushed the gagging boy down to his seat.

"What happened here?"

One of the boys pointed to Richard. "This old geek just tried to off Cory, here. And he wasn't doin' nothin'!"

"Yeah."

The driver turned to Richard. "What do you say, sir?"

Richard struggled with the return to himself. He turned to Jason and was shocked by the watery look of fear in his friend's eyes. "Take my chum and me to the park," he said.

"I say we shit-kick 'em right here!" The boy spoke again.

The driver turned on the foursome and pointed to the rear door. "Out!"

"Aw, what the fuck!"

The driver pushed open the exit. "Get off the bus, now."

Richard stared hard, unseeing. The boys filed away, the last one turning before going through the exit. "Fuckin' grody old weirdo!"

At the Stanley Park loop the bus stopped by the hot-dog stand near Richard and Jason's favorite spot. The two dismounted and walked slowly toward their bench by the lagoon. The sun was still on it, though the afternoon was now late.

"You missed it?" Richard motioned back at the parked bus.

"Missed what?"

"The action. I was forced to exercise a young 'un there who didn't know his manners. You missed it?"

"I missed nothing."

"You're fairly silent about it."

"What do you want me to say?"

Richard was stopped. His feelings turned firm. "You were never around when the real fighting was taking place."

"Now, now . . . "

They walked slow and easy to their bench in the sun. Richard looked through distant trees at a nearby apartment tower.

"I can see your old place."

"Eh?"

"Someone's put a plant in the front window."

"Needed something."

"I never thought so."

"For the love of God, man!" Jason was as animated as Richard had seen him in decades. "Will you never lie down and let the world change?"

Richard thought for a second. "It's come too ugly for me, Jason."

"Don't be a fool." He gestured with his hand at the trees, the pond, children throwing bread to ducks. "Look at this splendour."

"I see it."

"Does it look to you like a sap trench?"

"Of course not."

"You see then . . . "

They sat for a time, watching.

"Richard, do you never think of the war?"

"Seldom as I can."

"Do you still think of Vivian?"

"Every second. Until just now, on the bus. Forgot her for an instant."

"I still think of the war."

"I pity you."

The old men stayed for a respectable time watching the ducks, the pond and the children.

« 1986 »

Expo was a big success for the Vancouver area, bringing in tourists by unprecedented numbers, commerce and prosperity, noise and commotion. As with every big project which impacts a whole city, not all people affected were benefited. In that year and in those preceding, Richard lived by himself, still fierce to the independent maximum, in a small apartment in False Creek. The mega-celebrations were visible from his front window, the sound of extra vehicles, people and the attractions clear from his TV-watching couch. All this he accepted grudgingly and in the knowledge of its temporary-ness.

The trouble was with the fireworks. Every night at a few minutes after eleven the rumbles would begin, then vibrations from the charges resounding and reverberating with disturbing impact against the concrete of Richard's building. At that time of night Richard would be trying to sleep. Several times in the month of May he lurched awake while flinging himself across the little bedroom, his body instinctive, seeking cover. He would wrench himself out of the closet, stumbling among shoes, muttering and not immediately aware of himself. He tried to get used to it. But there was no mistaking the air-violence of a timed cordite blast in the near vicinity. Entertainment for some. To others a reminder of blood long-ago flung to the air.

So this and smoothness of the SkyTrain and the good

connections to downtown and his shrinking pension per-
suaded Richard to move to a cheaper apartment in Burnaby.
Here he was aged almost eighty-nine years, reading an issue
of TIME magazine somebody had left on the seat. So often
nowadays he was amazed. So many things seemed crazy. He
couldn't believe it sometimes. Though he prided himself at
expecting change he still couldn't believe it.

He looked at a picture of Madonna, a young girl who
painted her lips like Vivian used to in the 'forties when they
were going out for dinner on special occasions. Madonna
wore underwear like Vivian's too, only on the outside, or
by itself. Madonna sang confusing songs about being selfish
and proud of it. The other seniors at the Lodge felt this was
ridiculous. A scandal. Richard had no opinion either way.

He looked closely at the picture. In the young girl's half-
closed eyes he could see, if he looked carefully, something
familiar. It was clear she was remarkable, having come a
long way on what they said was nearly nothing. There was
a certain look of the face. Richard felt good that he almost
understood her. He knew that he would never try to
explain it to the others. He hadn't had a conversation
involving complicated matters like this in years. He thought
of Jason. Dead now for two years.

Richard often wondered now about the length of time
he'd been around, rode public transit, built houses, loved
his wife, battled madness, fought the war. He allowed himself to be philosophical about his years. He was in awe of the
fact that he had lived about as long as anyone had a right to
expect. He was allowed to think now; he knew it wouldn't
drive him insane like it once might have. It wouldn't make
him vulnerable to enemies and concerted violence. The
thoughts he had were softer now, less terrifying.

Nothing of the killing, thank God.

Looking through the wire-reinforced windows of the train he thought of the asylum. Madness was about as far away as the war was. The vibration from the wheels of the car through the upholstery and into his body felt wonderful. He knew he would make it to his stop in plenty of time for his renal system. He smirked to himself about that. God how long is this going to go on?

When he got off the train it was dark, a wet November evening, and he clutched his overcoat near and mumbled to himself about having opted wrongly for the lighter one he had instead of the good heavy model he'd gotten two winters ago.

Ah well, easier to walk.

Away from the station, having made his pit-stop, Richard walked haltingly among the houses, older in this section than others around. He was reminded again of his years. This was an untrammeled forest when I started building houses. Most of mine are older than these now, and they're tearin' these down now to build bigger ones. Heh.

He proceeded, warming with the movement, through the streets and toward the park that was his shortcut to the Lodge. Amid forested landscaping Richard paused to rest on a secluded bench.

The lurch to ground was as hard as any fall he'd had over recent years when his knees failed him or he misjudged stairs. Richard knew instantly that he had been sleeping with his face on the grass and saw the bench aside him. He stared at it by the bad light of a far street-lamp and knew that this was not an innocent fall. A movement by his head telegraphed alarm. He remembered a sobering roughness.

Cold contact with the ground. Amid duress, Richard contacted the old instincts. His attackers, shadow hitters in the gloom, became dread-creatures, too close and too free for safety. The park grass and the earth below filled his mind with musky trench-memory. Inside him the killing grew, heating a ball in his stomach, glowing outward to extremities of hot-powered violence. He rolled, certain, and regarded his adversaries in silhouette against the stars.

They ignored his movement, muddling with looted pocketbook and key change, sloppy and cursing.

Richard uttered last words:

"I know I'd kill you fellers if I could."

In an hour the deserted park held only one resident: The melted Richard Delta. His penetrated overcoat clutters at unevenly aligned shoulders and blood makes its dye job plain over much of what we have come to know as a man determined to serve his own way. Richard's jaw has been broken off and flaps loose within the skin of his ruined face. The skull is flattened, shattered by stomping impact which has spun splinters of porcelain-white into the surrounding grass. The damage is as extensive as any he'd seen in the great conflict and as he slips away he tries to shut away the willful irony of the long-held feeling that he might have deserved such a fate anyway, having dispatched so many others in such ways not dissimilar to this. But then there is no reason to consider such ridiculousness and his spirit is wondering if it can crawl across this park under cover, avoiding the shells and bullets, keeping out of sight and moving ever forward, unstoppable in the fatal gloom toward objectives not known.

The effort is as full as any Richard has ever attempted but his crushed structure fills with mysterious resolve and grasps the last potential from each of his molecules and wills his derelict remains forward through the grass. Seeing through squashed eyes, not feeling the pain of a destroyed face, his arms and legs broken almost off, strive without pain through the dewing undergrowth. His flight low through the weeds and pesticide-smelling root tops of a hundred-thousand shoots of grass, Richard now traverses on flee-ing muscle and levitating sinew, arguing every movement, each centimetre of progress through great conversations of effort.

Hours and lifetimes and halfway across a scarred field and almost to the sidewalk of the parkland his back engirds with a surging chill of wonderful energy. His arms and legs are bolstered with extra-human solidity and rising is possi-ble with a new body—body of a boy, wrapped in khaki and puttees, black-booted and striding, armed and ready, confi-dently rising still over the black lonely terrain until he is leap-striding over gravel and cement and sending himself wild over the streets he is leaving, the strides now bigger and huge. A monster charging clanging mauling presence on the landscape—killing his way, port arms. A giant forever in every good loaded tool, every caring of people, each cell of loving bodies, moving forward: a particle of will clacking down the years in frozen darkness.

Fishboat

I made some excuse and didn't go to work and decided to go down to the fish market to wander around the boats tied up at the wharf. I needed something different, a change of scenery. Even if for only a couple of hours.

Besides, an idea was coming on, forming in my head, clamping on tight like a barnacle on my brain. Times were getting pretty shitty. Almost enough to make me make a move. That was what the idea was about—my next move.

I stood on the jetty and stared for a long time at a trio of fish boats rafted abreast, the three of them sharing one boat-length of the crowded float. A grey-whiskered fisherman was sorting lines on the middle boat. An old salt type for sure, skillful at whatever he was doing. Nautical. Weathered.

After a while I called down to him: "Your boat?"

He went on working and didn't look up. I was going to ask again louder when a scuffing sound came from behind and a young kid's voice: "Nope. Mine."

I turned. The kid, no more than eighteen, had a fuzz mustache and a coil of rope over one shoulder. His running shoes made squeaking sounds as he walked and he kept one eye on me as he hopped down the ramp to the float. He turned away and leapt onto the inboard boat. Then he stood on the deck looking up at me. "Why?" he asked, a skinny street-rat killing me with his non-seafaring image.

"No reason. Kind of a fan you know. Small talker. Potential wanderer . . . "

"Yeah?" He turned and stepped toward the outboard boat.

"You don't actually own it though do you? Your father must."

He stopped with a sneaker poised on the fine teak rail of the craft in question. "I own it. And there's no father around."

"Oh. Well. Good for you." I looked around. "It's just that I've been watching that guy." I pointed to the Salt still obliviously mending net.

"His name is Sal. He's a burnout I rescued from detox. Take a close look at him."

I did what the Captain told me. He was right. Sal sans gray hair would have looked natural in a rubber room. His pinstriped engineer coveralls looked like institutional issue.

"You could be right," I said. "He your crew?"

"You kidding? I need dependable guys for that. Sal'd freak the first big swell we hit. His circuits'd overload. Besides he'd croak if he couldn't get to the clinic every day."

"The clinic?"

"Yeah. Someplace where they take care of guys like him. I don't know too much about it. He's good with nets though. Doesn't get frustrated. Hasn't got enough con-sciousness to get pissed off and bored."

"Hmmm . . . This is interesting. How does a young guy

like you come to be a commercial fisherman with his own boat and everything?"

He smiled.

"Oh I kinda just fell into it."

"Oh yeah?"

"Yeah."

I shook my head and admired his boat.

"Why don't you come aboard and take a good look at 'er?" He kept smiling. "She's got everything you can cram into one of these babies."

I hustled over the inboard vessel and stepped onto the boy's deck. "I was waiting for you to ask me instead of being some kind of pirate, you know."

Sal's work was spread around him like a ripped-up road map mixed in a pail and spilled out onto the deck. I was careful not to upset the careful mess. He had yet to acknowledge anyone's presence and now I was closer I could see a blank little grin on his face. Content but devoid.

The kid stepped down a hatchway and called at me to come down. I stepped lively trying not to show awkwardness. A surprisingly long ladder dropped me into the galley, a dark, greasy smelling, cluttered place. The galley table was being used as a workbench. A cabbage-sized piece of oily equipment—I would venture some type of pump—was partially disassembled and laying on it.

"Have a seat," said the kid, stowing the rope in a locker.

"Thanks." I pushed a couple of floater cushions off the end of a bench and perched down.

The kid pulled up a stool. "So wha'd you say you were? Drifter? Wanderer type?"

"Oh I wasn't serious about that. I'm a social worker by trade."

"Social worker. I've seen lots of those. You don't look like one to me."

"Well actually I work with criminals. I'm what you call a parole officer."

"I've seen my share of those too."

"You're a little young. Probably it was a probation officer you saw."

"Yeah, it was one of those. You still don't look like one."

"What's one supposed to look like?"

"I dunno. Not like you."

"Okay, well . . . Short of pulling my badge, which I don't have on me, I guess I'll have to just ask you to believe."

I looked around. Laundry, mostly heavy-metal muscle-T-shirts, some dirty. Piled in two hills atop a real-life seaman's chest. The carving on the chest depicted a storm-tossed square-rigger and looked hand done.

"Well, " I said. "You don't look like a sea captain."

"Yeah well . . . " He shrugged, scuffling to the galley. "I haven't been at it long. Maybe next year I'll look the part. Wanna beer?"

"Sure."

He pulled the door on a large cooler and came back with two cans. We popped pull-tabs and drank in unison. The kid didn't sit back down. He said: "You wanna see 'er?"

"Sure."

Cans in hand we toured the ship. Aside from the lived-in clutter of the forward quarters and galley the boat was as orderly and carefully maintained as I could imagine possible. Stepping over Sal several times each, the kid and I looked at the stern lockers where the fishing gear was kept. Despite the high potential for things to be tangled, fishing lines, hooks, pulleys and weights of every size were expertly put away, ready for use. The engine room absolutely sparkled.

"How do you keep things so clean? I always figured it would be greasy and dark down here."

"Has to be clean. Machinery gets dirty, it gets cranky and undependable. Nothing worse than a machine that doesn't work just because it's dirty. I mean there's better reasons to have a breakdown y'know."

"Yeah," I said, trying to sound knowledgeable.

The wheel-house was only big enough for two people and two beer cans. Brass fittings on the engine controls and the old fashioned ship's wheel glittered like precious metal. "Looks like you've got a wheel made of gold."

"Huh . . ." He ran his hand over the fine wood of the chart table set to one side. "If it was, there wouldn't be much sense in working the boat. Just cut off chunks and sell it."

"But I guess you can't really do that, can you?"

"No. Even if it was gold. And even if the engine block was made of platinum."

"I guess we're talking about purpose here. Personal sense of mission in life. We all have to have one."

"Yeah." The kid looked square at me. "Funny you should say that though about the gold on the wheel. I thought the same thing when I first saw one."

"Hmmm . . . " I sucked on my beer. "There's something significantly relevant or relevantly significant here—I'm not sure which. I think it has something to do with life, illusion and reality."

"Uh huh. Maybe."

We finished our beers back in the galley and had another one. Between the unexpected pleasantness of the tour and the first effects of the beer I felt I was getting my sea legs. The kid was treating me like an old pal. I realized I didn't even know his name.

"Look ah, what's your name by the way? I forgot to ask."

"Donald. People call me Don."

"After the duck?"

"Huh?"

"Donald Duck. You are a water-borne creature named Donald, aren't you?"

"You bein' sarcastic or clever or what?"

"Geez. You didn't get much of a childhood, did you?"

"Nope."

"Sorry. I guess I'm in kind of a mood. That's why I'm down here. That's why I describe myself in such wish-washy candy-ass terms. I'm pissed off with myself."

"I can see why."

"Yeah, yeah . . . . Look Don, what's chances of shipping out with you sometime? I don't mean right away but when I've got some time."

"What? You mean for an hour's run around the har-bour? Or to fish."

"To fish," I said quickly, now genuinely pissed because he'd missed my meaning.

"You didn't say you were a fisherman. You mean real fishing. Not sport fishing."

"Yeah. Work fishing. Not play fishing."

"Got any experience?"

"Well no but . . . I think my heart's in the right place though. I mean I've been seriously thinking of changing careers someday and fishing or working on a boat is one I'd like to try."

"Ever worked on a boat at all?"

"No."

Don paused and scratched his head like an old salt. The first faintly conventionally nautical gesture I'd seen him make.

"Hmmm . . . " He smiled and looked like he was suppressing a laugh.

"What's so funny?"

"Nothing. Just trying to think what I'd do with a piker like you who never worked on a boat before, doesn't know anything about fishing and lived in the city all his life. Maybe doesn't know what the hell he wants to do. Can you make a decent cup of coffee?"

Though he smiled as he said this, young Don's words came out cold. I could feel now the blade of the kid's street smarts, the hard steel centre to him.

"Never mind." I got up, finishing my beer. "Guess I was dreaming anyway." I crushed the can a little with my hand and then searched for a trash pail.

"In the galley," Don said.

I got rid of the can and trooped up the ladder-way to the deck. Don was close behind me. There was a freshening breeze. Smells of salt water and creosote in the lengthening afternoon were strong in my face. The feeling of being out of my element was increasing. I felt an urgency to get off the boat. I stumbled a bit passing by Sal and swore softly out loud. Stepping onto the gunwale about to jump to the deck of the dockside vessel I turned to bid Captain Donald good-bye.

"So long. Thanks for the tour."

"You don't have to run away all mad like this."

"I'm not running away."

"You don't understand what it's like out there. You can't fool around. Not like on shore."

Half of me wanted to exit right then. Leave with dispatch and let the kid out of my mind. I turned to him. "So who's fooling around?"

"Aw, come on . . . " The kid set hands on hips. He looked away, then back again. "You say you wanna fish. But you don't have anything to back it up. People get killed fooling around like that."

"I'm sure you're right. But what makes you such an expert?"

Don moved closer and spoke quick and hard, as if his words would not come any other way. "Look, I might not look it but I been hanging around these docks and these boats for more than half my life. My third foster home was to this fisherman and he took me out when I wasn't even eight years old. At first I hated it, cried all day and he beat me because I wasn't doing any work and he did other things to me too. It was just me and him on that boat and he kept on taking me out for years and years. I tried to run away a whole bunch of times but he always found me and then it would be right back on the boat and out again the next morning.

"For years and years I didn't go to school or anything just learned how to use a boat and clean fish and wipe up puke from being seasick or from drinking too much rot-gut wine. When I was fourteen I knew everything I had to know about running a boat but still I hated it because I was always being forced. It wasn't the boat so much or the ocean or the fish, I just hated it because I was being forced, y'know? You ever had that feeling?"

"Yeah maybe. I think . . . "

"Anyway, the year I was fourteen the old man was drinking and beating on me worse than any other year. It was fuckin' awful and one night I just got fed up and slammed the guy over the head with a two-by-four and he went down hard and hit the deck with his head. I was never so fuckin' glad in my life. I carted him to the side and threw him over. It was night so he went out of sight right away but a few minutes after, I heard him come out of it and start shouting and hollering. I didn't care.

"I started her up and booted it away from there. We were way out at the time off the northern river approaches and there was no chance he'd ever be found. I just sailed back here and told everybody I'd been sleeping and he fell overboard. Everybody believed it because that's the kind of thing that happens all the time in this business.

"So the cops took me off the boat and into another foster home but I ran away after the first day. I hid out downtown. I found people who didn't mind letting me sleep on their floors and I found out I could make a living getting fucked up the ass like the old man used to do when we were out fishing but only I got to pick who did it and even got paid for it. And to make money I started dealing drugs. You probl'y know people who do that for a living but I did it to make a big score and I never used the stuff myself. So I saved every penny from the dealing and the hustling and I bought this boat last year. Cash. I own the whole thing. I fish when I want to and don't take it up the ass for anybody anymore.

"And when I go out there I'm a fucking professional, everything gets done right. And if you work for me you got to know what you're doing. And there's lotsa guys like me around who know how to do it and don't take shit from anybody. So there you have it. Nothing personal, man but I don't think you're the type of guy I'm looking for in a crew . . . "

The kid stopped for breath. I looked away. Sal still obliviously worked. Voices from the market and boats and docks ticked and rattled in a whispering jumble. A flight of cackling insane seagulls harassed a corner of the dock where someone had knocked over a garbage can. I turned back to the kid. Some of the heat had gone from his look but he still had a hard face. A dismaying place to find such young eyes.

"I think you're right," I said. "Thanks again for the tour."

On the way down the dock the scrappy flock of gulls flitted in my direction. Approaching, the disorganized flight gaggle instantly disciplined into no-nonsense flight. Someone was yelling and flailing the air with an oar overtop the strewn garbage. As the gulls passed over me about thirty feet up one of them shat a streaming white dart.

I was ready. Reading the path of the bomb perfectly I dodged with plenty of time. The goo splatted in the exact spot I'd been occupying but I was far away. Far enough away not to get any shit on me.

Toba Inlet

One time me and a whole bunch of other guys, Sea Cadets, went on a sailing trip up the coast. Up to Toba Inlet. It was April and colder'n a bastard. Sometimes it even snowed and this is while we're sallying around in open sailboats and camping in borrowed boy scout tents. This strange thing happened I want to tell you about. It happened one day in some weird cove somewhere, way up there. I could never find it on a map now it was so long ago. Anyways we sailed into this place and it was like driving into a wall of solid rock because it looked like there was nowhere to go and just before you figure for sure it's game over and you're gonna rip the bottom right out of the hull a narrow crack opens up and you can sail right in and a small channel opens up. The channel opens up toward the end and forms a big cove, completely protected from all weather.

We pulled up to the far end where there was a beach and dropped anchor and went ashore. By the time we got setting up camp and cooking some supper it was getting dark but a few guys figured they'd go for a hike just to see what was around, y'know. Well, I was just sitting down to some beans and hot chocolate when a couple of these guys come running out of the bush and yell that they found something and another bunch of guys jump up and follow 'em back into the bush.

I was pretty tired so I decided to just sit there and relax 'cause some yahoo is always finding something on those kinds of trips and I was dead bored from looking at deer tracks and bear shit and all that stuff but soon the whole camp emptied out and I figured I'd better get in on what was going on.

It wasn't too far up off the beach in a clump of fern and hemlock trees that there was the entrance to a cave. I went in and crushed up inside a crowd of fellows squeezing against each other looking at something against the far wall. I weaseled my way up to the front and there was this human skeleton, perfectly bleached white, sitting against the back of the cave like some kind of high school biology display. One arm was lying tangled in the pelvis bones and the other hung around a big rock, like the guy had died hugging this rock as if it was somebody he knew. There were no clothes or nothing, just bones and everybody just stood around and gawked and then an officer turned up with a camera and started taking pictures.

Everybody'd been standing off just a little ways for a while but after they got used to the cave and more flash-lights got turned on they stepped up to the bones real close and one smartass reached up and touched the skull. He didn't hit it or nothing just touched it but the skull teetered and fell off the spine and rolled across the cave into the crowd. Really freaked everybody out for a minute there. But pretty soon everybody was moving in on the thing and grabbed pieces and after the novelty went away from it guys got their kicks running around with the skull propped on their heads in the dark for a while but nobody cared and really how juvenile can you get anyways?

Next morning I noticed the bones had been pretty well scattered. There were guys still playing with the skull. The cook was stirring a big pot of oatmeal with a tibia and getting a hell of a laugh any time somebody realized just what he was doing. Over at the end of the camp there was a waterfall and some jackasses were taking a shower, just standing there in the cold in their underwear but one guy had the ribcage and most of the spine down to the pelvis and he was pretending to dance with it under this waterfall. Everybody just about got sick everytime this twit leaned over and pretended to kiss his partner and then back it up against a rock and pretend to hump it.

Over by the mess tent some officer was drilling a hole in the breastbone, making a pendant. The whole place had gone skeleton crazy. I didn't give a damn about the bloody thing and I was plenty pissed off when the CO said we'd be stopping over for a day and sailing the next day. I didn't bother with the bones myself but maybe you noticed in my room, the lump of something that props up my dictionaries? Well, I'll tell you how I got that.

Later in the day we were all standing around the campfire trying to get warm. It was snowing or sleeting or something and the clouds had moved in low and boxed us in with the mountains on either side. It was getting late into the afternoon and some guys started having an argument and it began to get quite serious and look like a fight. They went on and on and all of a sudden one of 'em gets up and yells you sonofabitch and grabs a femur, a big leg bone, that had just been sitting around by the fire and clobbers this guy. Then somebody else yelled and wrestled the bone away and clobbers him right back. Meanwhile the first guy to get clubbed struggles up from the ground with his head bleeding away like crazy and dives at the other guy and pretty soon we got a total free-for-all going.

I got away from there like fast but before I could disappear someplace away from all the yelling and fighting something smashed me in the back of the head. I must have lost consciousness for I-don't-know-how-long because when I got back on my feet with this bastard pain in my head the fight had moved from the campfire on over to the mess tent and the officers' quarters. There were guys on the ground wrestling away and there were others running around picking up pieces of bone and chucking them at people. One guy hurled the skull at the CO who was standing there yelling for everybody to quit and it hit him hard in the side of the face. The CO went down and as the skull bounced away the jawbone cracked off and hit somebody else in the eye.

I looked down and there was this piece of bone, part of a foot I'm pretty sure, lying on the ground and it must have been what hit me. Anyways I grabbed it and this funny feeling got to me. I couldn't help it. I wanted to throw that thing so bad I don't know why. I ran over to a clump of guys and took aim but got knocked down before I could let it go. Somebody stomped on my chest and knocked the wind out of me for a couple of minutes and I thought for sure I was gonna die. I couldn't hardly breathe for a long time but I started crawling for the nearest tent and before long it was dark but I managed to get inside this dumb tent. It had no floor and the sleeping bag inside was pretty wet but I crawled inside, holding my guts 'cause now I felt sick.

And I was still clutching this piece of bone. Outside the guys were still yelling and every now and then I'd hear some shouting and a scream or two from the bushes or down by the fire, which was out. I didn't get much sleep because of the pain in my head and gut, and the fighting went on all night. Toward morning it got real cold and the fighting died down and I dozed for a while. Then I woke up and it was light out.

I looked out the flap of the tent which was half-collapsed because some assholes had fallen against it during the night, fighting. But I got my head out there and it was snowing again, cold as hell. There were people all around, some with their clothes half torn off. Lying on the ground shivering, some sleeping, some passed out and there was a few who had crawled over to the fire and were trying to light it again. I looked up the slope toward where the cave was and then I saw the skull. It had rolled down quite close to the tent and sat upright. It had a crack in it now and a small piece missing and it sat upright, facing me, looking at me. Snow was beginning to collect in the eye sockets and you know how skulls always seem to be grinning? Well even with no jawbone this bastard was smiling. At me.

After that everybody seemed to have snapped out of it and come back to their senses and we cleaned the place up and started apologizing to each other. Some of us who weren't hurt too bad went around and collected the wounded. There wasn't anybody dead, I don't know why, but there was lots of broken arms and legs, cracked ribs and there was even a guy with a fractured skull, hurt real bad. We had to get him to a hospital fast so that ended that trip and as far as I know they've never tried it again.

Funny thing nobody can figure out just what the fight

was all about or just why everybody had this overwhelming urge to scrap. I can't figure it out. Anyways we all got back okay and I found out later one of the officers sent a bone or two to UBC for analysis. Word was they were Spanish and not native like I kind of expected they might be. It's funny too I'd almost forgotten about that cruise even though I still have my souvenir, that bone that hit me, that foot bone. Came from almost the other side of the world hundreds of years ago and ended up giving me a terrific headache for a day-and-a-half way up in Toba Inlet.

Gas Tank

I'd known my legal secretary girlfriend for five months. She was before the waitress one and after the one who was a nurse. I was used to her skepticism but had not grown to like it. The best I could do was ignore it. She looked at the van, ran her fingers along its dusty rear window and gave me the look. In her sourness of face there was at stake my mini-vacation, so I knew ignoring her would not work.

"You kidding?" I hork-laughed, play-sarcastic. "This thing is German-built. Those people are compulsive freaks. Absolute fanatics about detail. These things run forever." I unlocked the side door. It slid open with well-oiled assurance.

"And look how comfortable it is inside. It's got a double bed, a refrigerator that runs on gas, a closet over here on the side. There's even an upper bunk that folds out under the canopy."

"It's so old."

"Tried and true."

Despite the pep-talk I could see by the darkness around her eyes that her doubt endured. We stood on the sidewalk outside the apartment, bags and equipment piled around us.

"It's crazy to leave so late on a Friday night," she whined.

"I couldn't get the thing until today."

"Why can't we wait 'til tomorrow?"

"And miss the sunrise? You don't know this place we're going to. It's beautiful. We'll miss all the traffic and in the morning you'll wake up to a gorgeous sunrise on your own private mountain lake."

She pulled the passenger door and slid inside, tugging lightly on a piece of loose upholstery.

"Did you have it checked by a mechanic?"

A chunk of foam stuffing came away in her hand.

"By the time I got it licensed it was too late."

I gently took the foam rubber away from her and went to chuck it in a city trash can.

"It's okay, though. I had a pretty good look."

She stepped back out and leaned against the sliding door, arms folded, eyes downcast.

"I don't know."

"Come on. Is that any way to act? We're on vacation. You know how crazy I'm going. Around this city. I gotta get away."

"I know . . . but."

We stood. Her leaning. Me standing. Both with arms crossed trying to out-pout one another. Just over three hours driving and we'd be there. I thought of the open road and the sound of quiet by the lakeside. She shifted weight from one foot to the other and sighed so I could hear it out loud.

"Get in," I ordered, taking a chance and getting the bags.

Underway in the 10:00 PM darkness dull familiar landscape flashed by: A black-and-gray dream-print of daytime life. In the colour version—the daily routine—I would drive this freeway on urgent or mundane business. This night it felt good to zoom past my regular exit and head further, captain of my own rolling ship, with a woman, a weekend's grub and a bottle of wine cooling in the gas-powered cooler.

The motor hummed along pretty good but with an occasional cough climbing hills.

"Needs a tune-up," I remarked.

She did not answer, but yawned.

"Driving in the dark makes me sleepy," she said. "Think I'll go to bed."

She yawned again and crawled toward the back. By the rearview I watched her take clothes off and put a nightie on. She brushed her teeth and spat in the little sink.

"Goodnight," she said, lying down, covering herself with the comforter lifted from her own bed at home.

I wheeled on into the night, full of energy. Sleep was the last thing on my mind. The further I drove the more right I felt about getting out of town. You have to get away once in a while. Recharge the batteries. I was going nuts back there.

Two hours later I pulled off the freeway and onto a secondary highway and went about ten klicks to our last turnoff, a rough gravel track into some low hill country. I hoped I could find the place in the dark. It was a couple of years since I'd been up this way, but I recognized a few landmarks. The midnight moon, almost full, helped a lot. It was good and lonely in this landscape. Just what I was looking for.

The driving got treacherous but I was still having fun. The road narrowed in places to a thin path up against sheer cliffs on one side and steep drops down black-hole gullies on the other. Then we started the long pull up a hill I was sure was the last stretch before the lake. I shifted down to second and let the van find its own comfortable speed for the slow climb. I ignored it at first but then there it was, a cough. Two coughs. Then several. The motor faltered and lost revs.

"Fuck." I remembered my friend in back, hoping she was deep asleep.

The motor recovered slightly, then took a big pause, coughing. Then it was dead. The van decelerated quickly on the upward grade and I stabbed the brakes to keep from rolling back. The headlights faded yellow as soon as the engine died. I realized it was a little chilly outside, and shivered a bit. Stopped in semi-dark I noticed the quiet and for the first time did not appreciate it. There was a heaviness about it, silence like death.

I pulled the hand-brake and switched the ignition back on, hoping for a miracle. Nothing . . . And only a tiny luminescence in the oil gauge where there should have been bright red dashboard light.

"What's wrong?" Her voice was soft but definite from the darkened rear.

"I think there's something gone in the electrical system." Our voices were impressive in the heightened quiet. The ticks and cracks of the cooling engine were audible beyond any I had ever heard before.

We sat in the roadway for a while. I kept watch in the rearview, fearing a speeding over-taker who might not see us in time and plow into our rear. After a minute or so this notion left my head. It was almost one in the morning and there hadn't been any other cars since the turnoff. Thoughts of an insecure night by the slanted roadway waiting for the dawn and a tow truck began taking sour form.

I released the hand-brake and let the van roll gently backward, turning the wheel hard over when I thought I had enough room, maneuvering the thing so we were facing downhill. I made sure the ignition was on and put it in gear.

"Gonna try a jump-start. Hang on."

Brakes off, it took only seconds to get going fast enough. I steered down the middle of the moon-silvered road, popped the clutch and floored the gas. Gurgling came from the engine. An alarming sooty smoke rose from the heating vents.

"What's that smell?" she called, still in her bed.

"Just the heating system. I guess it flipped on . . ." I hoped this didn't sound too much like the pure bullshit it was. "Smells like it hasn't been used for a while."

There was no sign of life from the engine even rolling as we were in gear down the steep grade. There was even less light from the dashboard and gooey fumes were flowing inky from the vents like airborne liquid shit. We rolled to the side of the road as far out of the way of possible traffic as the cliff-side would allow. I jerked on the emergency brake and opened the door.

"Gonna have a look at it, Sweetie. Could be something simple."

Simple or no it would be impossible to fix because, I remembered, walking to the rear, I didn't have a goddamn flashlight. Not that I don't own one. I have several. I could even think of where they were. One under the apartment sink, one in the storage locker. I even kept one at the office in the lower right-hand drawer of my desk. But here as I raised the engine-hatch by moonlight and peered into the coal-black motor compartment I didn't have a goddamn flashlight.

And a useless exercise it was, peering around in there. I couldn't see worth a damn. I couldn't even see my hand when I reached in to check around where I thought the battery connections were.

My middle finger touched something seriously hot. I yanked back my hand. In that instant I realized I could see something . . . . In the blackness the main battery cable glowed red. It even crackled faintly like plastic from a cigarette package shriveling in a campfire. A burnt-rubber stench wafted upward.

"Can you see anything?"

Her faint gravel-crunching steps sounded beside me. I looked away from the glowing wire. She stood in her nightie. The moon-bright lit her face and wherever the cloth did not cover, making me think of a metal statue.

"Yeah." I tried to sound calm. "It's electrical."

"Can you fix it?"

"You kidding?"

"What are we going to do?"

"Looks like we're stuck."

"Oh no . . . "

"Oh no is right. Thing's gonna cost like a bastard."

"I told you."

"Uh huh."

I leaned in for another look, hoping the appearance of constructive activity might keep her quiet. My eyes were getting used to the dark and this was no time for recriminations. I could see the darkened ends of the wire where it wasn't so fire-hot. Burned wires stretched everywhere. I felt around and found a loose piece of metal next to the battery.

"Fuck me!"

"What is it?"

"Part of the battery mount. Rusted to rat shit."

I felt around some more. The battery had fallen over, my hand told me it lay almost on its side against a mess of wires by the engine mounts. The gravel-jostling ride must have worked it free and caused a power-blazing short. My fingers were getting singed. The heat and burnt-plastic fumes sickened my head, canceling out the fresh mountain air around us.

"Just fucking wonderful," I said aloud.

One second later things were even more wonderful. A merry tuft of orange flame introduced itself from somewhere behind the carburetor.

"Oh! God . . . " She stepped away.

I lurched away and fell back to watch the wicked flare spring from one position on the motor to another. Panicky, I crab-walked rearward thinking the thing was going to explode in my face. Then realizing I might have to move faster, I scrambled to my feet.

"Have we got a fire extinguisher?"

"Are you kidding," I almost laughed. "You're talking to a man who goes camping in the deep dark faraway woods without even a goddamn flashlight."

I ran to the front for the water can stashed behind the driver's seat. Not that I thought water would do any good, I'm not that stupid. But what do you do in a case like this, anyway? I opened the nozzle and sloshed it at the engine. The water moved the flame back and away from where you could get at it, ending up somewhere down and under. To see where it was coming from I had to crouch under the van and stick my head up against the bottom of the frame. This I did without thinking, knowing the fire had to be put out or who knew what the hell was going to happen. I wedged myself further under and tried to get the water-can to a position where it was useful. I almost got completely stuck, my head firmly wedged between gravel and the rankly sweating gas tank. Great. I couldn't move the water can and knew instantly it was over.

"What are we going to do?"

The inevitable question. Probably heard it on every second TV action-adventure she ever watched. The worry in her voice was realistic, though. No television actress ever quavered like that.

I struggled myself out from under the van. The flames were now big enough to make the ground around us visible. In the licks and flashes you could see every stone and twig for three metres around. The occasional high pebbles in the gravel cast long, flickering shadows.

"It's gone to the gas tank. We better get back."

I took her arm and tried to just walk away calmly but then an audible whoosh sent a warm breeze past our ears. We lurched to a run for several strides before turning around to see the bad news. Fire was eating the entire rear of the vehicle, flames leaping up, clawing at the back window. It did not take much imagination to see where this night was going. I almost lost myself in the bitterness of it and only barely thought about what to do. For a second I was relieved that we were both safe. Then I remembered what all was in the vehicle.

"Holy shit, " I said, clutching my back pocket. "My wallet!" I felt around in my jacket. "It's in the glove compartment."

"Forget about it!" She yelled, backing further away, eyes wide. "You can't go back in there! It's going to blow up!"

Before she could finish I had run to the driver's door, jumped in and reached at the glove-box. A weird orange half-light glowed from the rear but it was still dark around the dashboard. After rummaging blindly for a few seconds, sweating, I found the wallet and whipped it into my jacket. Straightened in the seat, about to jump out, a strange impulse grabbed me. I paused, listening to the cracking and expanding sounds the van was making. There was something peaceful in it. The orange glow on the sun visor, the last there would ever be, recalled a thousand sunsets. Vibrations came up through the seat, almost like road rumblings, as if we were still under way. There was a tired, rending sound. A slow-easy metallic yawn. I got out, not hurrying.

"Thank God you're out of that thing! What took so long?"

Her voice jolted me.

"Couldn't find it at first."

"Is it going to blow up?"

"Dunno . . . "

"It always does on TV."

We soon had our answer. Moving back still further, the heat now too much for our faces even twenty metres away. There was another whoosh, bigger than the last. This time a white and red firestorm seared forward under the van, sending a shot of liquid fire five metres ahead. It looked like someone down the line of van-owners had bought the flame-thrower option, meant to barbecue anything in front of you in a traffic jam. The fiery tongue left the whole vehicle alight. The spare tire, mounted on the front, began to sizzle and flame.

"Oh God, oh God, oh God . . . "

She was beginning to break down. Standing there shivering, the steady fire-glow accenting the more fetching aspects of her night-attire, she eyed me with a mad glare. I took her in my arms, her face pressed tight into my shoulder. We stood, she sobbing, me watching the van burn itself to death. It was one of the more incredible sights I'd ever seen.

"Hey, you should watch this . . . " I realized I was taken with it and felt proud of having let things go and seen the little bit of fascination in all the shitty circumstance of it. "I mean, there's nothing we can do about it so we might as well enjoy ourselves."

Her face stayed buried, she said nothing.

"Haven't you ever wanted to set fire to a car before?"

She withdrew from hiding and wiping her face on my jacket. Then looked. The fire burned so bright that the woods around us were lit as if for a movie shoot. The moon paled and went invisible behind a massive plume of black smoke. Oily clouds gushed from the open doors and poured urgently from the rear. The smoke was so thick its condensed weight forced it to the ground before rising dispelled into the sky.

A giggle rose from my stomach, I could not hold it back. Shocked at myself, I tried stifling the hilarity developing inside me. It was impossible, like trying to keep ten thousand stand-up comedians from getting out.

"What are you laughing about?" She turned to me. "How can you think this is funny?" The tears had stopped.

"Aw c'mon. Look at us. There's gotta be something funny about this. I mean, look at that thing! Look at that sucker burn! It's like it just can't wait to burn itself to a cinder. Just burnin' its rusty little heart out . . . "

As I spoke a rear tire exploded, tossing chunks of sizzling rubber over the road. The sharp boom reverberated off the hillside. Another explosion blew the windshield out, molten shatter dumped like scalding rain onto the gravel.

As quickly as it came my humour was gone. I was jolted by a different hysteria. Picking up as big a rock as I could find I charged at the hulk and hurled it hard. "Burn, you fucking shitbox. Go ahead and burn!" The stone bounced away with an insignificant thunk. I picked up another and charged again, destroying the one window still intact.

"What are you doing? Don't go so close."

Though her voice rose above all the other noise I barely heard her, consumed as I was in a concentrated rage. But I did turn away, feeling relief on my hot face in the chill air breezing up the hill. I went to her and touched her arm and we walked a little further down the hill. When we turned back to it, the fire had climbed to its fiercest. Everything was burning, even the windshield wipers.

The windshield wipers for fuck sakes! I couldn't help but pick up another rock and run toward it, hurling.

"Stop it! STOP IT!" She screamed, almost out of control.

I picked up another stone but didn't throw it. I turned to her. Eerie light, the stuff of horror movies, surged from behind me and lit her in deep red and orange hues. As I approached, she screamed again and ran down the hill away from me, then turned off the road and struggled up the hillside. I turned to face the beast and saw why she had screamed and run. It wasn't because of me. It was because the thing was beginning to roll down the hill toward us.

There was the squeak of burned-away brake shoes. It moved sluggishly at first, lurching weirdly off its blackened launching pad. The spot was littered with soot and smouldering rubber. The wheels squeaked louder as it got going, the breeze stoking the fire higher and brighter. The beast left two smoking black ruts in the road. Two more tires exploded. A flaming shock absorber fell off and rolled to the side, sending its own dark column skyward.

The van gained alarming speed despite the blown tires, floating on its carpet of fire, an angry butterfly, flopping doors fire-breathing with the ride. It came faster, steady in the road as if piloted by a fire-ghost. I stood in the road, watching it come. My legal secretary screamed from the hillside as it approached, heating my nose, the sound of its lumbering clear and getting horrible.

For a romantic second, an image came: One lone man. One flaming recreational vehicle. Squaring off in the middle of the street. I flung my rock through the blasted open front and lunged to the side as the thing snorted past.

Workers

« ONE »

Toward dirtsteam's urgent punch of cleanswept skies the worker traffic fouls the road by pickup fumes and cyanide cigarettes. Men and women vehicle the road and wind through entrance gates to their world of standing sitting mending feeding tending and loading. Taking off with product and transporting. Their bodies they know as tools. Their minds they may not know so superfluous. The worker John enters the clutter driving an import and pouring hot liquid by the enormous thermos. He is expert in nonspilling. To grasp taste in a splash of face the faraway production. Breathing the final moments before factory entry as his time more sweet than most many moments of the days.

In the plant interior John plays to the work area. A warehouse of things to be placed and moved and nearby a rest area with long table and benches. Rows of lockerwalls and colleague Allen sits at table newspaper-reading.

John ends with a great thunk of thermos on table and speaks:

Jeeze . . . thought I was early. You always here this time of the morning?

The older workmate looks up from his newsrag and neither smiles nor otherwise and starts to speak then stops and finally does say these words:

Sure. Like to read a bit before work. Besides, the wife kicks me out before seven-thirty. Says it's easier to clean house that way. Now tell me what all that means to you.

Shit. You're lucky. My old lady hardly cleans the place at all.

She works, don't she?

Yeah.

Well, smarten up then. Y'gotta do yer part. She can't do it all. I wouldn't like my wife to think she had to do it all.

You gotta be crazy. I wouldn't take that kinda shit.

You haven't been married much. Wait twenty years.

Christ! Why would you wanna be married that long . . .

Whereupon our John gets up and goes to locker and grunting pulls coveralls to put them on.

Allen has given up the newspaper to put aside amidst diaphanous crackling. That why you're early? he says folding. You have a fight with er?

How in hell do you know everything all the time?

Like I say . . .

Before full marital philoso-crystalline comes forward is Allen interrupted by the arrival of game and husky Carl. Noisy. Smiles.

Hi everybody!

Air assumes energy as Carl booms the large voice. Trains his multi-wattage beam about the room. In seconds though he twigs fades thinks stops regards the sombre pair John and Allen.

Whoa. Like an everyday funeral home in here.

He handpelts John vigourous back-pounding.

Knock it off.

Oh!

Without stopping.

Sorry!

Not in the mood.

Aw . . .

What the hell are you so damn happy about? Whattya doin here so early?

Wasn't getting any sleep.

Bench groan-alarms by Carl's happy weight. Allen sits avoiding communicable attitude. Dourness darkens the face and eyes in rutted moats darkening still as he regards interloping chipper Carl. John joins by sooty stare and seats across-table. Idle grab of Allen's wrapped-neat tabloid.

Broad wouldn't leave me alone.

Carl sighs ocean-deep and ears perk. Expecting curiosity. Silence.

Man you shoulda seen this babe. The tits on er!

Uh huh. Disgusted John dumps paper.

And I suppose you been screwin er all night, eh?

What else you do with a chick like this? Shit for brains but man what a body. And hot? She was grabbin at my crotch all night. Couldn't believe it. Then she asks me if I wanna come back to her place for chrissakes.

Shit. John's hand unscrews mammoth thermos and pours. You probly squirted-off in your shorts and lasted about three seconds in er.

Oh no I got a strict rule. I do er with my finger I do er with my tongue. She comes twice or three times before she even sees a cock. Less of course she unzips me and starts

foolin around with it. That case I can't be responsible . . .
Oh man, you should see me. Don't know where it comes
from, but show me a good lookin babe with her legs open
and I'm Superman. Fuck like a mink all night! So hard you
could chisel stone with it . . .

Allen slams meaty open hand on table and laser beams
mortal blackness in Carl's skull.

A full day's work round here too young fella! Nuffathis
pornograph shit nonsense.

Whatsa matter, Al? I do my share . . .

Yeah, maybe. But old man Ainsley's in a bad mood these
days.

Mention of which makes Allen look feeble where
instants before his words raged a methodical vengeance.
Old man fumbles in coveralls for smoke.

I hear production's down . . .

Shit. . . . To the floor John spits. Word and mouthy dew
reaching boards simultaneous.

 . . . And management's gonna start crackin the whip.

Allen's fateful-large hands mutter with the match. Ignite
the stick. Hold to end of mouthtalk-bobbing cancertip.

They're gonna be crankin up the switch . . .

Bluesmoke by holes from Allen's face. Brow twitchfur-
rows and hacks rise from depths beyond body smoking and
wretch a gobby phlegm sentence. Verbal illegibility.

They'll be . . . (Hork) Firin slackers . . . (Hack-a-hack-
a-hawwk . . .)

Carl anger-hardens face.

Who you calling a slacker?

Easy (Hack) young fella.

Further cigarette depthdrag. Through graven smoke
speaks Allen.

Save your fight for the job.

I'm no slacker.

Allen crave-smokes. Lungfilling. Intoxification. Noseveins pulsegrow. Eyes blood. Gaze floorward in a gutcrouch holding his side.

Tacit interlude to Carl equates agreement.

Just ask ol' Johnny here.

Is all you guys can talk about is work?

John scowls a grimace more acrid than Allen's facial exhaust.

Fuck me I'm gettin fed up just sittin here.

Carl impshrugs. Gets up. To locker.

Silence.

Allen smokes death-respect quiet.

John uncorks further thermos.

Carl hops to the table. Overall-clad.

Anybody got the time?

John pulls anachronist-pocketwatch. Examines large time-hands with certitude.

Twenty to eight.

Thanks. Hop-returns to locker.

Yeah.

John speaks. New tone.

We're gonna be out working in a little while. Nobody get too anxious.

Carl fingerfumbles locker lock. Brow-wrinkled at the piece not looking up to talk. What the hell's with you today? Dialspins like Vegas neurotic. Old lady cut you off or something?

Never mind. Listen to me . . .

But fractured is John's vital sermon by materialization of workman Jerry. Carries likelarge coffee container suitable to ocean voyaging. John first-notices presence.

Jer! God, I'm glad you're here. These guys are driving me nuts.

Carl whirls. Finished lock-dicking.

More like the other way around, man . . .

Curly bright Jerry sits to unfurl a full smileforce on his stern toilmates.

What? Somebody picking on the great Johnny? My one and only biggest and best friend in the world? Lemme at em. I'll rip their tongues out and roast em for lunch.

He chuckle-unscrews thermos. Pour-aim steady without looking.

That's my man . . .

Carl looses energy. Slouches and mounts foot on bench to cradle chin in hand.

Good to see somebody's not gonna be a bitch all day . . .

Jerry ignores this comment. Gestures to John with the javatub.

Want somma this, Johnny?

No.

Carl seats. Allen pulls a board and they commence cribbage.

Jerry transfixes pal John. Glad it's Thursday. One more to go . . .

Yeah? Big deal. Blink your eyes, the weekend's gone.

T'aint that bad . . .

Yes it is.

Tired of workin, huh?

Maybe.

What else you gonna do? Kids gotta eat. Wives gotta buy the latest gladrags. What about all the things you want? Gotta pay for the toys, Johnny.

One way or another, I guess.

Sure . . .

Doesn't it get to be a little ridiculous when you look at it? I mean, here we are, pissing our lives away, working in this shithole to buy stuff that somebody in the same pickle is producing for the same purpose of paying for the toys that he's in hock for. Then there's a guy like Ainsley, sittin in that office with his hand on the goddamn switch. He wants us working faster, he just cranks a little on the switch and we go faster. The faster he wants it the faster we piss our lives away. It fucks my head, the whole business . . .

Turns conviction eyes blaring to the cardplayers. Listen to what I'm sayin Carl. No amount of fucking in the whole wide world'll change what I'm talking about here.

Carl ignores bleating missive. Outward signs tell he's heard similar in the past.

Jerry slaps knee in mock incredulity and in play camaraderie lays fingers on John's stolid arm.

So early in the day, Johnny. My brain can't take it.

Don't gimme that crap. You thought about it. You got brains but you don't use em. You even went to university for chrissake.

Don't mean batshit these days.

Has to. Should, anyway. Why the hell you quit halfway through and come work in this dump?

Use your head, John.

Up from the game Carl looks eager to share fifty wisdom cents worth in his eyes shining.

Knocked up the ol lady, morn likely.

Shut the fuck up, Carl.

Naw, nothing like that.

Why then. You never told me.

I did. You weren't listening.

I am now. Let's have it.

Nothing spectacular. Just didn't think I was getting anywhere.

That's like every other desperate sap in this sorry shithouse. You're different. You got savvy . . . or something.

Carl again.

Yeah, you got a lot on the ball there Jerry. Maybe have a doctor look at it.

Laughter.

What about last week when you dropped that box on old Billy's foot, eh? Old fart's still limpin.

He was limping a long time before that, says John. From the booze mostly.

Look who's talking.

I said it once and I'll say it again. Shut the fuck up loverboy or I'll . . .

Peacemaker Jerry interrupts. Take it easy. Besides, Billy and me got an understanding. It was an accident . . .

Too nearby a buzzer drills ears and kills conversation such as it is. Allen disinters watch from smoke-shrouded clothing folds.

Right on time.

All excepting John rise to lockers. Don coveralls those who have not already.

Yeah, right on time. Snarling John. Nother two minutes and all the mice go work for their cheese.

Clambercladding his work gear Jerry sniffs.

Is your head ever packed with shit today. What happened? Another fight with Karen?

Don't wanna talk about it.

John pours still another steaming torrent from tankard. Gulps in one pull.

Jerry finished dressing moves to table.

John still bartends another coffee for himself. Friend peers at his busy cup.

Funny lookin' swill you got there.

So?

Crazy asshole.

Sombrely listening the other men turn.

So surprised? Scowling John eye-lining his Jerry. We been working together long enough . . .

You're right. Gonna get yourself fired . . .

Who cares . . .

Maybe you don't but . . .

Gimme a break!

Grim John looks around. Scowls at others and back at Jerry.

Do you have to spread it around?

No. Everybody knows already.

Buzzer drills again. Fatal finality. Moves workers' nervous systems motioning involuntary upward and out. Clear lunchrooms in sound of steeltoed boots the plant over. Hundreds of shoeleathers contacting cement and rough boards. Noisy-strided through doorways. Purposeful emptying of sanctuaries. Carl and Allen don workprotector hard hats. Exit with factory flow.

John does not move.

Mygonna have to carry you?

Don't you worry.

John struggles astand. Wavers willowlike in imaginary breeze.

I'm a whirlwind.

Hardhats great eggshells fit and complete the dress ritual so complete action must immediately follow. Neither can just sit with brain protection on. Steeltoes echo through door and across warehouse. John and Jerry not speaking but move knowing they are overdue at workstation.

Scurry.

John cradles blessed thermos. Special places in a niche place in the wall near the John and Jerry "office".

Boys pull gloves. From someplace away conveyor belt extends and terminates with large level-mounted rollers. Urgent-large scared-red ON-OFF button mounted in plain sight and easy panic-reach. Cardboard boxes on belt for when button is pushed. Movement down the belt. Two forklift pallets positioned either side of the rollers. Industrial system.

John poises cladded finger over important button.

Nother day nother dollar. Eh Jer?

Conveyor rumbles calm like running water. John and Jerry commence employment. Taking boxes off rollers. Loading boxes onto pallets.

This they do and do and do and do.

Boxes generate source-unseen down cascading belt from up high. Continue at constant rate always and forever. Ever and ever without end.

These two men work but Jerry works and works and works while John just works and works. They heft. Lifting. Torso twist. Heft another load. Load. Twist. Heft. Load and twist and heft.

Then rhythm. Tossplacing. Twisting and tossing. Heft and lift. Tossplace. Lift. Twist. Toss and heft. Tossplace.

John pauses.

Why haven't we been replaced by a fuckin computer?

Ain't one dumb enough.

Heft and lift. Tossplace. Etc.

Jerry heftbreaths. Works and speaks.

Specially for you. (Heft.) I'm tellin ya Johnny. (Tossplace.) Don't knock it off it's gonna be (Heft. Twist.) game over for you around here.

John lampoons. Gonna be over (Loadheft.) round here . . .

I'm not kidding . . .

John works a basic blues of emergent rhythm in the work and words and workthought.

Da daaaah da-dum. (Heft.)

Seriously . . . (Twist.)

Da daaaah da-dum. (Toss.)

They riffwork. John blues-sings:

Gonna be over round here. (Heft.) Da daaaah da-dum. (Twist.) Boss gonna git sore round here. (Tossplace.) Da daaaah da-dum.

Not that . . . (Lift.) Too early.

Naw. (Heft.) Da daaaah da-dum.

Not in the mood.

Da daaaah da-dum. (Twist.) Don't worry about it. (Load.) I'll start. (Lift.) Da daaaah da-dum.

No.

Da daaaah da-dum. (Lift.) Come on. (Toss.) Da daaaah da-dum.

Shit . . .

Da dah da-dum. (Toss.) Spoilsport.

Awwww . . . (Heft.) Da dah da-dum.

Woke up this mo-nin.

Da dah da-dum . . .

Fell outta bed.

Da dah da-dum . . .

Had a big hard-on.

Da dah da-dum . . .

Pole-vaulted instead.

Da dah da that's awful! (Heft.) Truly bad. (Lift.) Didn even scan. (Tossplace.) Told you it was too early . . .

Da daaaah da . . . (Lift.) You do better. (Twist.) Da daaaah da-dum.

Man . . .

Da daaaah da-dum. (Lift.) Good start. (Twist.) Da daaaah da-dum.

You are a pain (Twist.) in the ass sometimes . . .

. . . Da daaaah da-dum . . . .

. . . I mean it . . .

Da daaah da-dum. (Toss.) Keep goin.

Woke up this mornin!

Da DAAAH da-dum . . .

Pain in m'ass.

Da DAAAH da-dum . . .

Saw my friend Johnny.

Da daaaah da-dum . . .

Knew it would last.

Da ha ha ha . . . (Tossplace.) Now we're rockin!

Da DAAAH da-dum.

Woke up this mornin.

Da dah da-dum . . .

Looked at the wife.

Da dah da-dum . . .

Knew I'd be workin.

Da dah da-dum . . .

The rest of my life.

Da daaaah dah-pressing . . .

Woke up this mornin.

. . . Daaaah da-dum . . .

Went down to eat.
Da daaaah da-dum . . .
Head was still spinnin.
Da daaaah da-dum . . .
Coon't find my seat.
Da daaaah believe it . . .
Been drinkin so long now.
. . . Daaaah da-dum . . .
Can't find my prick.
Da daaaah that's bad . . .
Wife's gettin mad, says . . .
Da daaaah da-dum . . .
No good fuckin' dick.
Da daaaah da-dum . . .
Da-dum. Da-dum.
Da daaaah da-dum . . .
Da-dum. Da-dum.
Da daaaah da-dum . . .
Woke up this mornin.
. . . Daaaah da-dum . . .
Pain in my head.
. . . Daaaah da-dum . . .
Juss can't help feelin.
. . . Daaaah da-dum . . .
Rather be dead.
Da daaaah da-dum. (Heft.) Da-dum. (Lift.) Da-dum.
(Twist.) Da daaaah da-dum. (Toss.)
Da-dum. Da-dum. Da daaaah da-dum.
Went to the doctor.
. . . Daaaah da-dum . . .
Said I feel bad.
. . . Daaaah da-dum . . .

Doctor said oh boy.

. . . Daaaah da-dum . . .

Isn't that sad.

. . . Daaaah da-dum. (Toss.) Da-dum. (Heft.) Da-dum. (Lift.) Da daaaah da-dum. (Twist.)

Can't get this achin.

. . . Daaaah da-dum . . .

Outta my back.

. . . Daaaah da-dum . . .

Boss sees me slackin.

. . . Daaaah da-dum . . .

Gimme the sack.

. . . Daaaah da-dum. (Twist.) Da-dum. (Tossplace.) Da-dum . . .

John and Jerry toilsong swing. Strophes producing clever momentum and so goes the work as is the idea of singalong activity and they hope that it carries them through to lunchtime swinging.

Workers uni-sing:

Da DAAAH da-dum. (Work.) Da-dum. (Work.) Da-dum. (Work.) Da DAAAH da-dum.

Da-dum.

Da-dum.

Da daaaah da-dum.

Da-dum.

Da-dum.

Da daaaah da-dum . . .

John beams with idea. Belts. Workweaving to task-energy:

Workin so hard now.

. . . Daaaah da-dum . . .

Can't get a rise.

. . . Daaaah da-dum . . .

Used to get so hard.

. . . Daaaah da-dum . . .

Won every prize.

. . . Daaah ya sure . . .

Da-dum. Da-dum.

Da daaaah running out?

Da-dum. (Work.) Maybe. (Work.) Da-dum.

Da daaah da-dum. Da-dum. Da-dum. Da daaah da-dum.

Went down to breakfast.

. . . Daaaah da-dum . . .

Got really PO'd.

Da daaaah da-dum . . .

Pancakes were burnin.

. . . daaaah da-dum . . .

Coffee was cold.

. . . daaaah da-dum . . .

Da-dum. (Work.) Da-dum.

Da daaaah da-dum. (Work.) I got a good one.

Da daaaah da-dum . . .

Opened my lunch box.

. . . Daaah da-dum . . .

Found lottsa mould.

Da daaah da yuck . . .

Cheese and the crackers.

. . . Daaah da-dum . . .

Past two weeks old.

. . . Daaah da blech. Da-dum. Da-dum. Da daaah da-dum. Woke up this mornin.

. . . Daaah da-dum . . .

Went to the john.

. . . Daaah da-dum . . .

Took me an ex-lax.

. . . Daaah da-dum . . .

Started singin this song.

. . . Daaah da-dum . . .

Finished my breakfast.

. . . Daaah da-dum . . .

Came in to work.

. . . Daaah da-dum . . .

Pain in my stomach.

. . . Daaah da-dum . . .

Just had to burp.

. . . Daaah da erp. Da-dum. Da-dum. Da daaah da burp.

Started to work.

. . . Daaah da-dum . . .

Just like a jerk.

. . . Daaah da-dum . . .

With none of the perks.

. . . Daaah da-dum . . .

Can't sit an shirk.

. . . Daaah da-dum . . .

Ass in the dirt.

. . . Daaah da-dum . . .

Like Johnny the twerp.

. . . Daaah da clever . . .

Da-dum. Da-dum. We through yet?

Da daaah da-dum. One more.

Da-dum. Da-dum. I'm tapped.

Da daaah da-dum. Da-dum. Da-dum.

Da DAAAH da-dum. Da-dum. Da-dum. Da daaah da-dum. Da-dum. Da-dum. Da daaah da-dum.

Boxes keep comin.

. . . Daaah da you're not kidding . . .
Right down the line.
. . . Daaah da-dum . . .
Feel like I'm dyin.
. . . Daaah da-dum . . .
In three-quarter time.
Daaah da-dum. Da-dum da-dum.
Workin for dimes.
. . . Daaah da-dum . . .
Isn't it fine.
. . . Daaah da-dum . . .
To work in the mine.
. . . Daaah da what . . ?
Run outta the rhyme.
. . . Daaah da-dum . . .
That kills all the time.
Wish you were mine.
It would be fine.
Give us a sign.
Mind in the grime.
Slinging the slime.
Walking the line.
Blowin the mind.
Whispering pines!
One of a kind.
Give up, for chrissakes!
Never! You started it.
Am I sorry . . .

Thus they work and resume under the factory din.
Thoughts the only music now. Fun period glow fades quick.
Steam into smoke.

Boxes heavy.

Guaranteed effort and warranted monotony a patented soulkiller. John in minutes goes to thermosbottle. With extraneous effort Jerry grimaces now. Glowers at John's gulping.

You gotta cut that out.

(Gulp.) I know.

Do it then.

(Gulp.) I will.

When?

Don't you ever want to fade away? Don't you ever have days you can't take it?

Sure. Think you're special?

You never show it.

It's there.

Ach . . . (Grunt, lift, twist.) I gotta start thinking about something else.

Like what?

Anything. To get my mind off.

Relax. You only got (Twist, toss, check watch.) seven hours and five minutes to go.

Big help.

Welcome.

Gimme a lead-in. I feel one comin on.

Another one?

Yeah.

Every day this week. A regular performer.

I gotta do something.

Whatever gets you through the night . . . or day.

Something good.

Let's see. We covered first car. First drunk. Best summer. Best car. Biggest fish . . .

Something fuckin good.

The best one's are gone unless you wanna do reruns.

I dunno. Today's real bad. Gotta be sex.

We did best piece'a tail last week. That was the third time.

Yeah. Hmm . . .

We ever do the first?

First. I think so. Maybe not.

Under the pool table in your best friend's rec room?

Naw. That was most fun in high school. There's another one.

Along think the boys with running-box rhythm of their lives. Pounding down coffee time and boxes keep forever guaranteed coming. Rhythm-echo of blues session still a gracious presence. Hateful killing toil gets past. Never waver.

One stretches a back a moment the other there to take the traffic.

Idea John pauses. Fingerpoints to head.

It's here.

Atta boy, man!

It's good. It's there. This story does not involve an actual fuck, keep that in your pussy-craving mind. Very important. Significant, you might say. Still gets me wondering . . . She was fifteen. It's the summer I turned seventeen. We can't take our hands off each other. We both feel it. It's pain! We laugh over it. It's unbelievable. The first couple of hours we're on the floor, making out so heavy our skin's rubbing off. We get on the bed and I reach around and start trying to unhook the unhookable. Fort Knox. No matter how I try I can't figure out the secret combination. Funny how in later life you pick up the skill, no problem. Back then it was hopeless. Finally she sits up and reaches round and it's done, zip. She wrestles it around under her shirt, flings it off and there they are, these two beautiful big tits under a thin layer of cotton. I still find that sexy as hell. A woman with a shirt but no bra on. I unbutton. I touch. I rub. I mop around with my tongue. Fantasyland. Pretty soon I just gotta slide my hand down under her pants. Down to where the elastic waistband is. And the silky-slick panty material. I stop there for a while, think I can feel a crack. I realize that part of the silkiness is wet. The place is wet down there. Really soaked. Oh man. I didn't expect this. I didn't know what to expect. Who'da thought she'd be sopping like that. The things you don't know. Unreal. So she's a little scared by now because maybe she can feel how slick she is and feels embarrassed or maybe she's not ready for all this or something. I don't know. But we keep going and pretty soon I'm under the panties and groping around in all that dark forest. Man oh man how I love getting lost in the woods. And sure enough I feel her wide open under my hand and I'm getting all wet too. And then without even thinking about it, without even pressing, my middle finger is gone. Swallowed. Slid into the quicksand. It happens so fast I almost get scared. I mean, I knew the basic facts. Enough to know that more than just a finger is s'posed to go in there but . . . I guess I didn't know how easy it can slide in if the little darlin is ready for it. I look back on it now I love it. But then, then all I could think about for a couple of seconds was, what did you do with my finger? I pulled it out, looked at it. Still there, not even a different colour or anything. I was kinda surprised. Disappointed, maybe. I expected something different. She's moanin and happy. What a feeling! she keeps saying. Baby, I says, you're not kidding . . . But I don't know if we mean the same things. I don't think so at all . . . Anyway, I've got the biggest, hardest, most painful prong-on I've ever had. Feels like it's gonna explode. Then she gets up and takes her pants down, flops on the bed and says she's ready. I don't need any more encouragement than that ol buddy. I get my shirt off, undo my pants and then it hits me. This fear. I don't want to take my pants off. I get on the bed. Lay between her legs. It feels great. We grind together a lot, getting hotter and hotter but I don't want to stick it in her. I'm afraid. I can't explain it, but it's taking a big step into unknown territory and I'm just not ready. I think of it today, hah, would I do it? Fuck me! Would I do it? She was good-lookin, too, boy, nice tits. Oh man . . .

Just couldn't do it . . .

Just couldn't do it. Chiming Jerry smiles. Step over the line . . .

Yup. That's it. Think it means something?

Oh probably . . .

Thought so . . .

Least it's one we haven't done before.

Good?

Sure. (Toss, watch check.) Ten minutes. Maybe more. Bit-of-a-hard-on, too.

Hah.

Which does me no goddamn good working on the loading dock like this.

Come on.

You crazy man . . .

You bet.

With which sweaty John deftly departs thermos-ward. Jerry whereupon workstops.

Come on, John.

Nonlistening John boxerpunches STOP button. Thunking wood. Whomping boxes lurch fishtailed like panic-stopped freeway cars.

You gonna pick at me all bloody day? (Gulp.)

Asshole. Production backs up Ainsley'll think it's both of us . . . .

Don't try and fool me. You don't give a rat's ass what old man Ainsley thinks.

Don't think so? You're gonna find out for sure because here he comes and you better straighten that pile.

Jerry punches button.

John half-hearts at straightening neatness. Scowls beneath-breath bravado. Management Ainsley approaches authority-stern.

Mock official John speaks pain-tone. How fast do think we're running today, Gerald?

Don't know.

Not fast enough. Ainsley mightyspeaks. Better be prepared to snap it up. This line is in for a smartening.

John stares. You gonna speed us up again, Mr. Ainsley?

Right you are.

Stare-John hardens. Wouldn't you be afraid of the guys wildcattin like they said they would last time?

Bout time workers in this plant stopped talking so much and put in an honest day's work.

Circumspectionboss inspects worker's loadwork. Talkturns to John: They really been talking like that?

Maybe not exactly. Lot of them are pretty hot about the last time we had to speed up. Couple of them mentioned wildcatting. Don't know if there's much serious business to it.

Snap-to Jerry finishes listening: Johnny's kidding, Mr. Ainsley. Nobody said anything like that.

Ah but they have. Yesterday a bunch down in the main lunchroom planned what they'd do if we had to go faster. Said it would spread from production on to the shops and down the warehouse faster'n you could heave a cuppa cold coffee out an open window, Mr. Ainsley.

Eloquence of Johnny-speech knocks with mystery-brawn. Ainsley momentarily impressed. Then thought and eyes narrow. Turnspeaks on John. Are you all with us here Watkins?

Jumpsaving Jerry to the fray. He's not. Are you, Johnny? You're tired. Trouble at home. Not much sleep, eh, Johnny?

Naw. I'm fine.

You're not.

Whatever. Off-backing Ainsley opines. Get it straightened out and keep working.

Yes sir.

Never to have end easily boss/employee encounters. Ainsley only begins to leave but thinkingly stops. Turns again to converse.

By the way. Since you hear so much these days. Do either of you know anything about the accidents last week?

Anger-joyful John enjoying his burn. Does not acknowledge.

Jerry pounces:

Accidents?

Maybe you wouldn't call them accidents. Number two machine went down. Twice in a week.

Feigning-John interests: Anybody hurt?

No. You know damn well. I just wondered. You're the talkative type. Anything to say about it?

Well no . . . Tries Jerry.

Grave-Ainsley grey-haired. Emburdened at silent Jerry.
John drops a box and lunges the words:

You talking sabotage? That what you're talkin?

Johnny!

Whatever you want to call it, Watkins.

Better watch what you're saying. Or the guys'll have this place stopped up like a constipated cow so fast it'll make your nose itch.

Keep your mouth shut Watkins. Pretty soon you'll be looking for another place to shoot it off.

Yeah . . . ?

Now total John and Jerry work definitely stopped. Glaring John catmoves slight toward bossman. Jerry punch-hits resounding STOP button. Relative silence lays stagey emphasis to goings on.

Quick-Jerry advances conciliatory:

John doesn't mean anything, Mr. Ainsley. He's not himself today.

He's damn lucky he's got you carrying him. He'd be out on his ass long ago.

He works hard enough, sir.

Why stick up for this bum? He's a natural slacker.

John bristle-growls:

One more word and I walk out of here. You won't get a chance to fire me. I claim harassment and the union backs me. My production record's right up there. I don't have to take your shit.

For chrissake, Johnny. Will you shut up?

Be wise to take your friend's advice, Watkins. Meantime, don't let me see you causing trouble. I mean it, boy.

Ainsley bossman quick-exits. Backward glance.

No words. Conveyor resumes. John and Jerry resume.

Insistent now backed-up boxes faster.

Why you suckhole to that fat sumbitch? You should tell him what you think. None of this yes sir right away sir crap.

Gotta keep workin's why. So do you.

Yeah sure.

Conversation turn nasty enough for John going again to thermosbottle. Mid-swallow sees old man in extra-dirty coveralls limp to their frame. Makes cautious progress to John and Jerry loading domain. Guides electric personal decorated handtruck. Life's special bumperstickers. Other stickable mind accoutrements and precious motorized thing carries boxes.

Cheery-Jerry swings hello:

Hiya Billy. How's the foot?

Stay away from me.

Elder stops. Emphatically points.

I wanted to tell ya. Stay the heck away from me. Keep your distance, young fella.

Unswigged-John returns from drinking wall.

Hey Billy. Afraid of us?

Him.

Jerry?

Yeah.

Aghast-Jerry working. Cheer-grimacing. Yelping fictional astoundment:

Billy! I didn't mean to drop that box on your foot. Honest. Sure.

Honest.

Like hell.

Sure hold a grudge . . .

Yeah whatsamatter Bill? Scared of your shadow these days?

You guys are crazy. Both of ya. Drop a box on my foot. Next thing I know maybe you swing on me with a baseball bat. You want my job so you try to kill me.

Jerry incredul-work deepens. Grimace-scowl breath-contorts with quickening of box arrival. John sweats. Billy backs off and makes to leave.

Jerry yells:

Come off it Billy. Joke, right?

Wrong . . .

Because of a lousy box on the foot . . .

Which one you guys slip that wrench in my machine last week?

Alco-breath John disengages. Smirk-laugh.

Shit. (Snort.) Not this again. (N'ya, n'ya.)

One a you guys did it. You got a thing for me a long time.

Non-pleasant John:

You're the one that's fuckin crazy.

I got the boss on my side. They know you done it. They gonna get you before you get me.

Aw Billy. You're all paranoid or something. We don't mean you harm. Do we, John?

Naw . . . We don't mean ya no harm . . . (Slipstepping John at Billy fakes enroute box to old man's head. To rightful pallet loading place.) . . . Least nothin an ordinary hospital couldn't fix up in two or three months . . . Eh, Jer? Hah!

Don't listen Bill. He's strange from working too long.

Billy ignores. Serious-setting face to task at mind. Steps to peck-box off conveyor. Both you guys . . . (Loads electro-truck cargo.) . . . are crazy. I'm out of here. Control-handles to blast off.

John taunts after:

Don't forget to check your machine. Hah!

Jerry work-talks:

Settle down. Made your big point for the day. Almost got us fired. Enough?

Whatsamatter? Don't wanna play too?

Piss off.

Oh . . . Da big man's gettin mad.

Fuckin right.

Darn. What can I say . . .

Enough for one day. Clam up.

Both do.

John sees askance at an approach. Here comes Mary. Clam up. She spreads everything.

Yeah. Crabs, syph, a little herpes simplex here and there.

Shut up!

Enters industro-female to load-stream. Clipboard. Papers. Lab-coat.

Hello, boys.

Boys, she thinks we are. Shit. She was still playing with things that rattle when we were gettin golden memories from darlings older'n she is now.

Odious as usual I see, Mister Watkins.

Why I thought I'd improved since last time.

Can't tell any difference. Anyway, you know where you can shove it.

Mary I'd love to. I wish you'd spoken up sooner.

Work-joshing Jerry shucks:

You two again?

John and me are good friends. We love insulting. He is an expert at verbal abuse.

After work, honey. I'll show you something about abuse.

Bet you could.

Find out.

Yuck. Even the suggestion. The thought of you makes me want to spew. You like my poem?

Provokable-John toss-drops box. Pistol-grips her arm.

You ain't nice, girlie.

Appalled-Jerry whereupon toss-drops load and panic-punches STOP button.

Are you nuts? Let go of her.

Mary and me are just having a little friendly tussle. Isn't that right, Mary dear?

Let go of my arm, Watkins.

Better do as she says. Before Ainsley gets back up here.

John semi-relents cocked grip.

Told ya before. I don't care what Ainsley does.

Armrubbing Mary never takes wary-glare from John The Belligerent. You should. I saw a memo today. They're thinking of firing you.

Why don't they?

The Union. Has to be good reason and your production is good. I can't imagine how . . .

So they can't fire me . . .

Not unless you do something stupidly serious like get drunk at work or something.

Hah!

Laughing-John's inebriation. Prances work area. Mimic steel-toe ballet steps with finger-end hardhat spinning. Imaginary self-airplanes about conveyor belt. Motor sounds above plant and conversation.

What's with him?

Gone weird today.

Weirder than usual, you mean.

Yeah. Actually, tell you the truth, he's been getting stranger every day for the last while.

You're not kidding.

Playing-John soccer balls hardhat. Dribbles fine across workfloor.

So. Anything new around the office these days?

Not much. You know about Baker's wife.

Oh yeah. She had a miscarriage?

Uh huh. But they found out she can get pregnant again.

That's good.

Propellerhead-John pokes between. Naw, that's bad.

What are you talking about?

Well it's clear, isn't it? Baker's old lady drops a kid then Baker's into this place for good. Gonna spend the rest of his life kissing Ainsley's ass.

Flies away anew. Buzzing box pallet over-swoop and away.

How long has he been like this?

All morning.

Cruising-John right back elevating over conveyor. Damn right, all morning! And all afternoon and all tomorrow and all next week . . .

Can't you do anything to shut him up?

I've tried.

He's tried!

AeroJohn takes imaginary flight off again with arms.

Any more news?

No. Oh, you heard about the new job they created?

No . . .

AirJohn soarswoop returns.

New job? We got enough of the goddamn things right now. We don't need anymore. We can't stand anymore . . .

Which job is this?

Bunch of things. They're going to wrap it all up and call it General Operations Manager.

Operations? Isn't Ainsley kinda the chief of that sort of stuff right now?

He says he's getting tired of it. The directors want him to hire someone to do what he does out here and he'll just have the office stuff to do.

John with away-wings. Ya know what that means, dontcha? Means we're gonna have two assholes around here stead of one!

Quiet John. What does it pay? Do they know yet?

I guess it would be something like what Mr. Hastings gets as Accounts Manager.

That'd be a good lot of cash.

Can't pay me enough to work in this pisshole.

John landtraverses wallward and thermos. Jerry punches conveyor start.

Work.

They're interviewing two men this afternoon.

Know who they are?

No but I saw one of the applications. Looks like they're having trouble finding someone qualified.

Ainsley's pretty fussy. Nobody's gonna be good enough.

John returns.

Hah. Well of course, Jer. The man is after all replacing himself!

Funny.

Thanks.

They want somebody pretty good. Production's been down.

Hah!

When do you think they're gonna make a decision?

Soon, I guess.

Wary-gazing Mary over shoulder.

Better go. Bye.

See ya.

John jolly-stumbles box in hands.

Hey baby! What about tonight, darlin?

Skirting Mary ignores.

Sniffing Jerry. Give it up.

Awww . . .

Work-resume up-paced to clear backed-up impatient boxline.

Hefting John (Twist, toss-place) labours more than before mockflight.

Oh man. These mothers get heavier. (Heft, twist, toss-place. Lift, twist, toss-drop.)

Gotta take a piss.

Go then. I'll cover.

Hey, Jer! I just had a great thought!

'Bout taking a piss? Hate to tell you, boy, but it's been thought, if you know what I mean.

No, no, no. Forget about that. What I thought was that you, my friend, should put in for that job.

Sure. Brilliant. Real smart. Specially considering you're snapped out of shape and it's only nine in the morning.

I'm serious. You got a shot. You got the time in. You know this place, for what that's worth. You got education . . .

Forget it.

No. Think about it . . .

If it's any comfort, I have thought about it. It's hopeless, see.

It's not.

It is. They're looking for some big-time exec.

That's a load of horseshit. A little jerk-off joint like this? Nobody's gonna come and work in this dump and order us grunts around and take the turd Ainsley hands out.

I don't know . . .

Come on. Know what they say, think positive!

Now you're talkin the load of horse manure.

Gotta give it a try.

What makes you so damn interested?

Somebody's gotta make it outta this dead-end dive. And I've always liked you, Gerald . . .

Shit . . .

. . . and you know I want to see you get what's best out of life . . .

Thought you had to take a piss a while back?

Still do.

Well when you go, tell Hans to get his ass over here with that forklift and pick these loads up. We're gonna be full soon.

You're always telling me to smarten up and shut up and get working and all that. Why don't you smarten up and go talk to Ainsley and tell im you deserve that goddamn job?

I thought you were gonna go for a piss?

In a minute.

Better not leave it too long. All the mops are down in the warehouse. Long way to walk with wet pants.

Aw, shit, Jer. Listen. You gotta talk to Ainsley. It's a matter of pride.

Pride!

Yeah.

Only one around here should be worried about pride is you. Gonna piss your pants in a minute.

No I'm not but I will if you don't talk to Ainsley.

Fuck off.

No. In fact, I'll haul it out right here and piss all over you if you don't.

You're fucking crazy.

So?

No.

Yes.

Fuck off.

You fuck off.

I ain't doin it.

Yes you are.

No I'm not.

I'm haulin out my dick.

Haul it out and jerk it off and throw it away. I don't care.

Here it is.

Put it back.

It ain't goin back.

It's an ugly fuckin thing.

Does wonderful things.

Not here, please.

Whattya say?

Besides yechhh!

Whattya say?

Flagellant worker-boys virtual-cease toil. Jerry looks at gelatinous-flaccid John-member bunched in latter's soil-knarled fingercoil. Gleamdripping head threatening hideous eroto-maniacal potential.

Finally: All right! For chrissake I'll go. Now put it back in your pants and go over and take a decent leak and tell the goddamn forklift to get the hell up here, okay?

Promise to talk to Ainsley.

I'll talk to him.

Promise.

Okay, okay, I promise. Fuck yes.

John flapconcealing jouncy truncheon. Whoopee!

For chrissake.

Bowlegged-John stepwalking to thermoswall. Extraworking Jerry hard-put to keep up with persistent boxes.

Returning-John gestures.

Hey. That fag hindu is coming.

Ravi's not a fag.

Sure he is. Ever see how he looks at us? Moves his eyes up and down all over a guy?

That's his way. Does that with everybody.

Brownman in question hoves-to carrying boxes.

Hey paki!

C'mon, Johnny. Jerry heft-twists. Gimme a hand here, they're comin faster.

Fuckin Ainsley with his hand on the switch . . .

Ravi pauses by workpallets. Mirth-considers activities going on.

What you say there, Wats?

I said hey paki.

Name not paki, prickhead.

What'd you call me?

C'mon, John. Call the forklift or help or something.

Box-characters come quicker now. Insist they be noticed. Serviced. Handled and placed. Jerry punchkicks ever-ready STOP button but weight and speed and ponderous conveyor forces continued stackup.

Darkness of box-plodding packed tightly down belt and falling off rollers in a suicide of overproduction.

Overworking-Jerry tries mess-control. Pick-boxes to floor around fulloaded pallets.

You deaf, Wats?

John grabtustles Ravi. Stumble-conflict past collecting products among which hapless Jerry-partner frets and despairs.

Nobody calls me names. Specially goddamn fag hindus.

Where the fuck is the goddamn forklift!

Fuck you, Wats.

I seen the way you wiggle around here, paki. Everybody knows you're a fucking fag . . .

Boxes stagleap rollers clutchbunching and friction-growling crowdedness in every place. Jerry surrenders.

Johnny.

Now amid nonresolvable imperative movement we might as well conscious-fade because there is no way out from our messes of machinery and anger-addled men.

« TWO »

Worksession in recess. To cocktail lounge-cum-cabaret-beer-hall workerboys retire. Smokesoaked. Pit. Such might find in industrial large-enough city of pollution and population. Belligerent blues-rock roars from speaker-multitude. Lynyrd Skynyrd and/or Allman Brothers. B.B. King. 'Tain't Nobody's Bizness (If I Do)'. Bar patrons power-drink and scowl and dance.

Inhabits our John a corner of this emporium with good

wives. Table-seated Karen and Sally before goodly number of full and empty bottles and glasses. Finishing John slaps latest jar to woodtop with authority.

For chrissakes, where's our order.

Acid-Karen tosses wifely derision. You haven't sobered up from today.

Aw, get off about today. My head feels like a piece-a-shit.

Innocence-Sally a charm amid ambient dirtknowledge. Her flute-voice among tubas.

You mean you were drinking already today? Didn't you go to work?

He went to work all right. And he took his little friend with him.

Lay off!

You're making a fool of yourself.

Should I leave? Uneasy-Sally shift-talks. You guys want to be alone . . . ?

Stay, Sally. This goon isn't going to be trouble. Not if he wants to live in his own house.

You sure, Karen? Maybe Johnny wants to talk this out.

Him? Talk? Hah!

Yeah, stay Sal. Jerry's gonna be here any time now. With news.

News? Query-Karen lightens.

Welcome subjectshift enhances Sally. Jerry's talking to Mr. Ainsley about a new job. Why do you think they're being so long, Johnny?

Maybe Ainsley wants to show ol Jer around the office. Maybe he gave him the job on the spot . . .

Hmmm. That's not the way it sounded over the phone. Jerry doesn't think he'll get anywhere at the plant.

Naw, he's a natural. A shoo-in. He can't miss, old Jer can't.

Karen softgazes husband approaching caring bemusal. Lips curl. Smirk. Eye spark.

What buds you guys are. Male bonding taken to near sexuality.

Huh? What the fuck you babblin about. An how bout those drinks we ordered? Waitress! Waitress!

Quiet down. She hears you.

Place isn't worth a shit for service anymore. WAITRESS!

I think she hears you, John.

Damn right she hears me.

Don't pay attention to him. What's this new job about, anyway?

Jerry says it's called Operations Manager.

Sounds good.

Good? Good? Damn right it's good! Goddamn great is what it is.

What does an Operations Manager do, Johnny?

How would he know. He'd have trouble operating a tomato plant.

Real funny kid, real funny.

Why don't you happy up a little? You're spoiling the whole evening.

You're the one that's spoiling things. You're the one who thinks I can't manage nothin. Well maybe I haven't been any ball of flame up to now but I think I got potential. Even if you got no faith in me I happen to think I got potential.

Stacking boxes and opening beer bottles doesn't take potential. What's next? Getting your own potato chips?

Cute . . .

Longsought waitress wished-for comes. Offloads drinks. Wordless departs. Sally cheers to the booze refit.

What do you think of all the good weather we've been

getting? I'll bet the boys are having a lot of fun with the new swimming pool.

They could if their father would plug the hole he made in it.

That wasn't my fault!

Mr. Know-it-all who never reads instructions. Drilled a hole through the bottom.

Waddn my fault, I tell ya. Stupid toys these days. No durability.

Humph . . .

Come now, you two. Surely we can find something else to talk about. How's work, Karen?

Same as always. I'll never get out of that place. We'll never have enough money . . .

Doncha think I'm tryin? You think I like seein you go to that dumb store every day?

Pondering-Karen while Sally elates and spies spouse across floor.

There's Jerry. Over here, honey.

Vocational activist Jerry sporting this night slight better clothes than ordinary. Sits aside Sally.

Hiya, babe. Came as fast as I could. Does Ainsley like to talk.

You're cheerful. How'd it go?

Yeah. Get the job?

Better than I expected.

Good.

That's wonderful!

What the hell ya mean better than you expected?

Well . . . It wasn't a big downer or anything like that . . .

You get the job or didn't you?

No.

Oh . . .

No?

I'm sure you tried, dear.

Yeah, I tried. But it was just like I thought . . .

Just like I thought too. Ainsley's a fucking prick-face. Goddammit!

It wasn't like that.

Son-of-a-bitchin bastard.

John, watch your language.

Lurching Karen. Yeah, can't you see there's ladies present you dumb shit!

Aw you guys ain't at it again . . .

They are.

Don't pay attention, Jer. She's got shit for manners anyway.

You son-of-a-bitch!

We better go . . .

No. You guys can't leave, not until we hear about that asshole Ainsley.

Not much to tell.

Come on, spill it. You been with the guy almost four hours.

He took me for dinner.

Whoop-dee-doo . . .

That's nice.

Where did you go? Someplace expensive?

No, we weren't dressed for it so we just went to the Longhorn.

Isn't that where a lot of businessmen go to talk over big deals?

Well, this was no big deal.

It sure as hell was! This deal was about whether or not

an everyday working Joe can get a break. This was big, all right. This coulda proved there's a chance for a guy to make it in this fucked up system . . .

It couldn't have proved a thing, Johnny, and it didn't. Except what we thought about Ainsley was wrong. He's not such a bad guy once you get talking to him. In fact, he's a lot like us . . .

Like hell.

No, really. The guy's got things that bug his ass, just like us. But, man to man, if he sees you've got something to say, he listens.

The bum buys you a steak and all of a sudden he's Mr. Sensitive. What about when he sits in that office and lays his sweaty meat hooks on that master switch of his. You think he cares what you got to say then?

Snortlaughing Karen. Will you give us all a break. You never had a conference with anybody more important than a liquor store clerk in your life. Let Jerry talk.

Conciliator Jerry. Let him go, Karen. He's having his fun.

Aw, listen to him. As if you're not ready to kick ass over this yourself. What did you an the boss do all night? Fall in love?

Enough, John . . .

Yer actin like some kinda faithful dog . . .

Can it!

The way yer goin we're gonna be gettin table scraps around that place instead of paycheques!

Real funny, there, fella. Why don't you take your wife's advice and quit so we can at least get a half-pleasant evening out of this . . .

Quit?

Booze-whacked John's distracted perspective contains argument but no words. Elucidatory anger. No punching-bag. No context. Snorts he: What the hell. You said yerself. I can't quit.

Not work, dummy. All that stupid babbling.

Why don't we dance, bubbles Sally. The music is great tonight. Jerry . . . ?

Sorry doll, kinda buzzed. Lemme have a drink and sit awhile.

Okay.

I don't know about anybody else but I gotta go to the little girls room.

I'll come with you.

Good idea, Sal. We'll leave these two alone. Maybe Jerry can calm this hulk down a little so we can have some fun.

Order us another round when you're over there, will ya?

I hope you brought some money. I'm broke.

I got enough . . .

Depart-women flaming as from carwreck.

Wistful Jerry. Company of disaster. Leaking anxious gasoline. You gonna cheer up tonight or you gonna spoil it for everybody?

I don't wanna spoil it . . .

Better come around quick, then.

Personal cheer effort Jerry takes wide slug of what is in front of him. Smacks. Satiously sighs. And what's the matter between you and Karen? I mean you guys were never the greatest love story ever told or anything like that but fuck me you're like a couple a wildcats.

No big deal . . .

Come on . . .

It's nothin. We scream and yell. So what?

That all?

Is that all what?

How far's it gonna go? How bad's it gonna get?

We're okay. She's okay. Forget it.

Uh huh.

Leave it at that, Jer. Anything else is none of your business.

Don't worry . . . Look, we been friends a long time.

Doesn't have to last forever.

Yeah, yeah . . . But look. We talk. We always sat for hours and gassed about the damnedest stuff.

Yeah.

No limit to the confessions, right? No secrets.

Right.

And it works good, too. Remember the time me and Sal were havin trouble in bed?

Yup.

I was uptight and pissed off and you started me talking and I told you what was the matter? How she used to just lie there and take it like it might as well have been a carrot sticking up her and I would get so bored I'd fight off falling asleep.

Yeah.

It helped to talk about it. You said I should make it more interesting for her. Jazz things up a little.

Smiling John at his eroto-mindscreen. Slamdrinks. That I did.

It worked! Did it ever. Nowadays I put a scarf or a tie or something around her neck and pull it tight but not too tight and say something like I'm gonna fuck you, bitch. Til you can't take anymore.

Does it to er, eh?

Better believe. Boy, you never seen a piece of ass so good now. Wears me out. The girl is so hot when she sees that scarf, she jumps on it . . .

Really did the trick, huh?

You bet, Johnny boy. You helped me out that time. We had some real sessions back then.

Yeah . . .

Break while drinks delivered. Wordless waitress offloads. Leaves.

Well what's eating ya then, boy? Whattsa matter? You're mopin around and making everybody's life a soap opera.

Aw, you know . . .

The work thing?

Yeah.

Well hell. You never been this bad . . .

It's been pretty bad . . .

You're telling me.

Bad inside. I can't explain. Feel like I'm dyin. Like every box I move in that place is taking a day off the end of my life. Can't shake it. I been having nightmares. Ainsley with his hand on that switch. Fucking us. Using up our lives faster and faster. Can't seem to beat it. Just can't climb up and walk away. We're stuck. Fuck me . . .

Johnny . . .

Forget it.

No.

I'll get over it.

Maybe you need some help.

What?

I dunno . . .

A shrink, maybe.

Maybe.

Ferget it.

I can't.

Well too bad for you. It'll start burnin holes in your guts like it is me. Take my word for it and do as I tell ya and forget it, okay?

Okay . . .

And tell me what happened with Ainsley tonight and cut the crapshit.

I told you. Nothing.

Bull. There's something else.

What else?

There is . . .

Mantalk stopped at depth as conspiro-giggling wives re-enter. Shortstopping Karen deadens by look of the boys.

Uh oh, seriousness . . .

Do you think we should leave them alone?

Lightened-Jerry. No, no. Sit down.

Girls waryseat themselves.

How are you now, sweetie? Relaxed?

Okay.

There's a bunch of your work buddies over there you know.

Uni-twisting boys at Karen's nodhead direction.

Carl and Mary and that East Indian guy . . .

Bunch a dildoes . . .

They're kinda fun. Asked us over. You guys for it?

We're talkin . . .

Talk, talk, talk . . .

C'mon, babe. Let us alone for a while. Just a bit longer.

It's babe now, eh? God Jerry what did you do to him?

Johnny's a real puff-ball at heart. A pussycat. Aren't you, Johnny?

Sure.

Oh, good. Now we can have a good time!

Nodheading-Karen strategically sights.

Hey, isn't that Mr. Ainsley coming in the door?

Uni-twist all to visual verification.

Yeah.

Just when things were looking up!

Easy, boy.

Who's that with him?

Got me . . .

That, my friends, is the new Assistant Operations Manager.

What?

Ainsley told me all about him. Name's Jeremy something. Just out of the Institute of Technology. Highest marks in the class.

Looks like a wimp, ya ast me . . .

Will you guys get your minds off work and have a little fun? Let's dance.

No.

Come on, lovey. Just a little one.

Forget it.

Pretty please.

You got something wrong with your hearing, lady? I said no and I mean it. You want some exercise, go get us some drinks.

You've had enough.

You're wrong.

Drunk-emphasizing John cocks drink. Chugsaway single slurpy megagulp.

I'm gonna need more.

Would you take me for a dance, Jerry?

Sorry, honey. I just don't feel like it.

Let's split this popsicle stand, Sal. These two are dull and loving it.

I don't know . . .

Come on, girl. There's good times waiting for us. Let these two figure things out for themselves.

Go ahead, hon. We'll be over in a while.

Yeah, you guys mingle. Send more drinks.

Departure-wives make toward workmate tableload. John and Jerry ardently avoid to look. Daggerglares John instead at separate Ainsley.

Whattdya say we go over there and plow im in the teeth.

You're talking like a madman.

Yeah? You're not comin off so sane yourself, my friend. How come you're so crazy about im all of a sudden?

I'm not. He gives me credit for being a good worker. He says I might have a future with the company . . .

Hold it. He just finishes dumpin ya—am I hearin' right?—for the Ops Manager job and hires that snotface over there and then, in the same breath, he starts talkin about your future? Shit. If it comes to that, hell, I got a future too. I got a future stackin boxes and swillin out the crappers. We all got great futures, kissin Ainsley's ass . . .

Oh shut the fuck up for chrissakes and listen for a minute. You been asking for it all night so I might as well give it to ya.

Gimme what?

The real reason I didn't get the job . . .

. . . Yeah?

You.

Huh?

You.

Whattdya mean . . . ?

Don't pretend. It's bloody obvious. Everybody knows. Everybody talks about it. That's why I didn't want to say. I'm your only friend down there . . .

What the fuck're you talkin about?

You been jerkin off and fuckin around at that plant too long, friend. You're unpopular. And anybody who sticks around you is unpopular too.

You don't mean to say old man Ainsley's so pissed off about this morning that he's . . .

It's not about this morning. He doesn't care. And he knows you were drinking, too.

Yeah . . . ?

He didn't do anything about it because he wants to get you on something bigger.

Jeersmiling-at-this-strange-juncture-Jerry weirdly knuckle-jabs Mr. John's ribs times numerous.

Kinda shakes the old cock-sure ballsiness, don't it, pal?

You're fucked in the head, man . . .

Maybe. If I am it's because I been trying to stand up for you all night.

I still don't know what you're talking about.

C'mon boy. What's been bugging management's ass lately? What's got em so paranoid they can hardly screw at night?

Take my word for it. I don't know.

Well if you're that stupid I can't help you . . .

They're not trying to weld that sabotage number to me?

Ka-CHINGGGGG!

I'll be fucked!

That's the idea.

Dammit.

Don't act surprised. You been a prize asshole lately. They know you're crazy enough to do it. Right now they're trying to get solid proof so they can fire ya. You been askin for it. I don't know why but you have.

Wait a minute.

Revelating-John rises and sternstands. Commandspeaks downward. What's your headspace on all this?

Sit down, Johnny . . .

Don't Johnny me. What do you think? Did I do it or didn't I?

Who cares.

Somebody. It matters to Ainsley or you would'a got that job. In fact, I'm gonna go over there and show that bastard how bad it can get. I'm gonna sabotage him. I'm gonna shove his teeth down his throat. I'm gonna rip his balls off.

Forget it.

Twistwrenching-John earcuffs-Jerry heavily away. Grip-Jerry pushrises with both hands. Forward-bearing pair off-footing both from sitting to standing. Boys chaircrash enroute the floor. Strugglwrestle amid spillage and sitwear strew.

Settle down!

Leggo, Jer. Whatssitmadder!

Strugglerising-John afoot with clingJerry kneebound. Grabhauling available legs. Movement-drawn Karen and Sally reappear. Accompanied by bemused partycommitted Carl and Ravi. Dancewalk none too apart and vaguely paired upon this muddlescene.

Laughbinded-Carl speechimpaired: You guys better get a better fight goin or the bouncers'll never notice ya.

Who asked you asshole?

Touchy, touchy . . .

Take it easy . . .

What'er you and that hindu fag doin with our o'ladies?

Somebody's gotta keep em happy, John . . .

AngerJohn whereupon stablunges Carl. Upknocks tablespray booze. Closefollowing-Jerry restraining John. Aimpunching-Carl at John's chin. Fight underway. Booziness of all concerned. General fighting skill comiclack. Conflict funnily violenceless. Womenconcern screams and actionavoidance. Jerry accepts Carlpunch and descends. John swingbacks.

Ravi backstanding at outset then swingjumps John. Onhangs. Backriding and careens with mount curtseying to pummelfind Carl.

Faggot raghead!

Women pushavoid and exittake.

Call a cab, Sally.

Angry fightsounds unresolvable. Suffice to know nobody dies this night.

« THREE »

Violence brings to a table-and-chaired kitchen and a windowed door and the other urbanstandard window through which housekeeping housemembers patrolwatch whilst dishwashing. Nightdark blanks these portals with but tinges of a somewhere-off streetlight.

Drunkssound mirthsinging stepheavys upon porch. Flicklight outside kitchen door. Jerry-faceform appears.

Lockfumbling and dooropening. Jerry and Sally. Karen and John.

Cheermaintaining-Sally shucks sweater. Volunteers:

I'll make coffee.

Scoffscowling John. Coffee. I need nother beer.

Steady-Karen. Coffee'd be great, Sal.

There's tea if you'd like.

Maybe that'd be better.

What a bunch a jam tarts. Come on, Jer. Let's have a beer.

Umm . . . I could go either way.

Come on, you guys. It's only three-thirty.

Watchchecking-Karen. Closer to four.

God, why do we do this to ourselves.

Teapotbusy-Sally. I know. Work tomorrow . . . I mean today. How do we do it?

I guess we're young and tough. Just like our boys here. Huh? Real scrappers these guys are.

Hah-hah-John.

Gutholding-bent Jerry. Oh . . . Think I bent some ribs.

Ah, buddy. You were beautiful.

Really?

You bet. The way you stood up to those bouncers . . .

We still got kicked out.

It was a great getting out of there. I'm glad we went to those other places.

Kitchenbusy-Sally. I should say so.

Anyway, I'm glad you fellows finally worked it out of your system what was bugging you. Nothing like a good rumble. Coupla cavemen.

My yes . . .

Hey you girls. Don't get me an Jerry here wrong. We don't fight cause we like it. We just do what we have to do, that's all.

Ooo . . . My hero. Talk like that always send shivers up my crotch. Take me home, you beastoid, you.

Ah, it's tough bein wild enough for you, baby.

Tangled John-and-spouse lustcoil writhing. Feign near-genuine passion.

Rising Jerry feignretches. Yecch, think I'll take this opportunity to go tap a kidney.

Hey, Jer. What about a beer?

Oh yeah . . . Rummagelooks refrigerator. Fraid you're outta luck.

No beer? What kinda place is this.

Who cares, honey. Let's go home.

Tea's on. Anyone like a snack?

Guess we could go out and get some.

Gone is then Jerry behind bathroom door.

Yeah!

No . . .

What can I get you?

I'll go out and get some beer.

Nothing Sal, just tea.

You'll have to go downtown at this hour.

That's okay. I'll take Jerry's truck.

Sure you wouldn't like some coffee? I can still make some . . .

He's got that look in his eye, Sal. Coffee's not going to cut it.

John doorknocks the bathroom.

Hey, Jer. Where's your keys.

I don't know if you should drive.

Nonsense. I drive like this lotsa times. How else would I get between bars. Hah.

Dooropening Jerry to toiletflush noise.

What?

Your truck. I'm gonna get some beer.

Oh. In my jacket.

Be right back.

Okay.

Do me a favour, Jerry. Go with him.

Okay.

Good. Get a cab. I'll call. At least now we know we'll see you hunks again.

Door-departing halfjacketed and yawning boys with tempered macho-send endearment from alert-Karen.

What a pair . . .

Yes.

Sally buswaits teapot to table.

They certainly stick together.

Thrumsound of starting motor revrunning. Gravelcracking vehicle-movement. Headlights beamimpress through windows and cancel.

Karen shrugsighs.

Can you believe that fight. I thought those people were friends.

Pretty nasty all right.

I don't know if its a particularly bad thing. No one got especially hurt. But why even fool around like that?

Men are strange.

I'm with you.

Like a cookie?

No thanks.

Women-pause in weight-thought like clerics.

John's been a scalded cat lately.

Jerry's been upset too . . .

Sally hurryswills teapotsteeping.

Karen perks. I think it's about that sabotage thing. Has Jerry mentioned it?

Uh huh . . .

What's going on down there? The two of them are like fleas on a frying pan.

Jerry says John's in a lot of trouble. He doesn't know for sure. He . . . didn't want me to talk about it.

It's okay. I got a bit of it from Carl. Some machine fouled up. They found a box stuck in it.

And they think maybe John had something to do with it. That's all Jerry told me.

That's all we need. That bum loses his job and we're tits up.

I hope everything works out. I'm sure John didn't do it.

Thanks Sal. Know what? Crazy as that man is I know you're right. John wouldn't go in for stuff like that.

I'm sure everything will be all right.

Yeah. I gotta say, your old man is sure bearing up under the pressure. Working with crazy John all day, going for the big job . . . He sure took that well.

He's been disappointed before. He's pretty brave but it kills me to see him lose like that. Wish I could do something to help him.

He's a pretty lucky guy to have a fan like you rooting for him.

I suppose . . .

Can I change my mind about the cookie?

Sure.

And I better call my sitter.

Use the phone in the bedroom.

Okay.

Telephonebound Karen up the stairs. Sally busies looking

for cookies and locates two kinds. Gets plate. Arranges display. Cookieplaces plate on table.

Calling-Karen from above. Whooee! Love your new bedspread, Sal. Cathouse Red.

Sally giggleblushes.

Reappearing Karen down stairs with shoulderdraped black silk scarf.

So this is the infamous Screwing Scarf.

Oh . . .

Fuck me, baby?

Oh stop . . .

Don't stop. Oh don't stop?

Laughsnatching Sally scarf away.

Quitit.

Jerry the famous Silk Scarf Lover!

Nobody's sposed to know.

I'm the only one you've told?

Yes.

Good God girl you should spread this around. Brighten up a world full of dull sex lives . . .

Tea-drinking Karen scarfwraps neck.

How does he do it. Like this?

You've got it around too many times. Unwinds and shows. Like this. Demonstration-Sally. And he holds it like this and the rest takes care of itself.

Like this?

A little tighter.

How tight?

Like this.

Severe-drawing Sally acute.

Hold it!

Undraws Sally's hands away.

Too tight. That was scary . . .

You think so?

Damn right. Does he do that with you?

Well . . .

Tighter?

Sort of . . .

You guys are into this worse than I thought. Do you like it?

No.

Then why?

It doesn't actually hurt. Jerry would never hurt me. Not on purpose. And it seems so important to him. I thought about it. I hate it but if it makes Jerry happy I'll do anything.

You got more balls than me, sweetie. John ever pulled something like that I'd go apeshit.

Women-silence eye-staring.

I'm glad I told you about it.

I know.

I wanted to get your opinion.

I know how it is.

Women-silence glance-away.

You guys ever think of having kids?

Lots. Jerry wants to wait.

We did that too. Then you get to the point where you forget what you're waiting for. I mean, you want to feel good about it and all that. You want to have enough money. But eventually, if you're gonna do it, you just do it. Having kids is like that. Was for us, anyway. It just happened.

Jerry doesn't like anything to just happen.

You can't plan everything, I don't think. I know one thing, those two little grommets of mine are all I care about in this world.

Your boys are sweet.

You bet. The best thing about it is if anything happened to John or we split up or anything like that they'd always be mine. No matter how bad it gets I always have them. A word of advice dear, always keep that in mind.

I will.

And I'd do a little thinking about this s&m stuff. In fact, a friend of mine had a problem something like this one time and she found this place downtown where women can go and talk to somebody.

Quietsitting Sally teadrinks.

Rising-Karen. Where's your phone book?

I'll get it.

Fetchfinding Sally. I think you mean the transition house.

Yeah.

I've heard of it.

Pageflipping Karen. They counsel women whose husbands have flipped.

I don't need it.

You never know.

Headlights impression the windows. Trucksound.

Alarmstop Karen bookclosing. We gotta talk more about this.

Yes . . .

Doorslams. Stairbound Sally with phonebook and scarf. Feetclumps on porch. John and Jerry into kitchen six-packs-laden. Prestarted John sports beer in hand. Tables beersixes. Emptyhanded nonscarf-Sally returns.

Jovial-John. Howdy there, ladies.

I see you haven't been depriving yourself.

No, my little sweetie-muff, I haven't. And thanks to the

cab-hiring skills of our man Jerry here, your brave knight returns. In one piece.

Small blessings.

My little sarcastic cherie, how's about a little snuggle.

Armwrapping-John to Karen in sloppy hug. Attempted mouthkiss.

Blecch. Hit-on by a drunk.

Smilebeaming-Sally. Would you like tea, sweetie?

Sure, babe.

Have a beer! Canripping six-pack John. Come on, Jer. Party.

Too tired to party.

Tired? Hah . . . Guess I'll just have to be Mr. Goodtimes by myself.

Well, Mrs. Goodtimes is tired too. (Yawn.) I'm going home.

Jeez . . . The party's breaking up here.

You mean to keep it going?

Sure, the night's young.

If it's okay with Jerry and Sally, it's okay with me. I know better than to try and interrupt Jumpin Johnny when he gets rolling.

Would you like me to drive you?

No, Sal. I'll walk. I need the air.

All right.

But call me tomorrow.

Okay.

Goodbyekissing women.

Beergulps John present can. Uncracks another and watches departing-Karen.

Fine woman, that one. Glad I married er . . .

First sensible thing you said all night. Even if you are kidding.

I wasn't kidding. She's the light of my life, my guiding beacon, my . . .

Stop!

Lightcutting-Sally off porch. Makes toward stairs. I'm tired too. Can I make you anything before I go to bed?

Naw, babe.

We're great, Sal. Thanks anyway.

Well goodnight.

Night.

Goodnight, cherry blossom. Sweet dreams . . .

Chuckleclimbing-Sally out of sight.

Good woman you got there. Super-duper.

Absentstaring-Jerry. Yeah . . .

Swigdrinking-John watches stiffstaring-Jerry bore eyeholes in table. Downsets beer emphatic. Hey. Earth to Jerry, come in . . . Whattsa matter boy?

Nothin.

If this is nothin, I'd hate to see somethin. Hafta give ya mouth-ta-mouth resuscitation.

Waverwalking John to kitchen window. Peers out. Wanders to kitchen clock. Timechecks against wristwatch. Attempts beer-in-hand chronowrist instrument adjustment.

Heavysighing-Jerry staring.

Returning-John downsits.

This bullshit about that job. That's not still buggin ya is it?

What about it?

I dunno. Just wouldn't want you to piss your brains out about it like I would . . . do, like I do. I mean, somebody's gotta be strong about it . . .

What's being strong got to do with it?

I dunno. Just . . .

What do you know?

C'mon . . . Don't get crabby on me. Have pity on a poor drunk.

Sure.

Besides. We're still buddies. No doubt aboutit. That bullshit tonight, fuck it. You're my main man, bro. Nobody takes that away from us.

Heavysighing Jerry repeats. Rises. Walkspeaks.

You'll forgive me if I don't find great comfort in that thought, Johnny.

I never known you to be like this. You talk like that . . . you don't sound like any friend of mine. Don't know if I should get mad at you or ignore what you said or what.

Try keeping your mouth shut for a change. Try it. Just for me, your main man. Try it.

Fuck me Jerry, I . . .

SHUT UP! JUST SHUT UP FOR FUCK SAKES!

Unnerved John backleans in chair. Stands.

I'll get goin, I'll . . .

I didn't tell ya to leave. I just want you to be quiet.

John sits.

Struggletalking Jerry. L . . . Look.

It's okay, Jer. You're upset. It's okay.

. . . Not okay.

Yes . . .

No . . .

Yes it . . .

Quiet!

Okay.

Handraising-Jerry. Sorry I yelled.

Shrugging-John.

I'm pretty fucked up.

My fault . . .

Uh uh.

. . . It is. I wasn't thinking what I was doin with all that jackin around down at the plant. I wasn't thinkin . . .

It's not that . . .

You'd be on your way now.

Not for sure. You can't tell.

I sure haven't been helpin ya out.

It's not even that.

What then?

Me.

You.

Yeah.

Howdya figure?

I dunno. I don't like anything.

Hell. Lots of people don't like things. Lots of people don't like a lotta things.

Naw, naw . . . I just fuckin hate everything.

Everything?

Everything.

What . . . this house?

Yup.

You hate your house.

Hate it.

Your new truck?

Hate it.

Boat?

Hate it.

Fishing gear?

Hate it.

That new roof we put on the garage?

Hate it.

In-laws? (Laugh.)

I'm serious. Hate em.

Taxes? (Hork.)

Hate em!

Job?

Hate it.

Life?

Hate it.

Wife?

Hate . . .

Sourscorning-Jerry awayturns. Seatshift.

Beerswallowing-John tipfinger nervetaps table.

Risewalking-Jerry windowward. So you see . . . It's a pretty fucked up scene.

Don't sweat it. You might not be as weird as you think. Relatively.

Whirling-Jerry to table. Armgrabs John. C'mere. Dragwalks John windowbound. See out there. In the moonlight. There's a lawn out there. One of the best goddamn lawns in the goddamn town. And you know what. I hate every goddamn blade of it. Every grain of fertilizer I ever spread on it, I hate. I hate my lawn mower, my tool shed. I hate my tools. Can't stand the thought of em. I hate the day I bought this place. I'm in a little trouble here. Hope you can see that . . .

I can, yeah . . .

Good.

Table-returning Jerry. Beeropens. Drinks. Know what it's like to hate your tools?

No Jer. Can't say as I do.

What about hating your tool? (Horksmile.)

Aw you old shitflinger you. You're kiddin me up the old wahzoo aren't ya?

Heh, heh . . .

Yeah you're havin me all the way up shit street you ass-hole!

Hah, Hah . . .

Horklaugh and beerslug and relaugh.

Smilefading-John darkens. Look Jer. We gotta come up with something at work. Some new goodtime scam. Relieve the boredom. Give the guys a thrill and a laugh . . .

Blow up another machine?

Facetwisting-John necksnaps. What made you say a thing like that?

Nothing. (Pause.) You're right. But what.

I dunno. We'll think of something. Long as we're on it, you and me, we'll come up with something.

Yeah . . .

Let's join softball this year.

Naw . . .

We could come on like a coupla madmen.

Naw.

Come on . . .

Cajoling-John reachbunts Jerry playboxing.

Boys play.

Punchplay gets vigorous. Standmove at roomcentre chucklefighting. Aimlanding Jerry scores a few at John's midsection.

Not there . . . Gotta take a piss.

Clinchwaltzing boys a second. Then slowstop. Clasped. Solemnhugging.

Then break face-on. Mutual forearmholding.

You're a good buddy there, Jerry Sparman.

You too, slugger.

Fuck, lemme go . . . Gonna piss my pants.

Not this again.

Hah, hah.

Backing-Jerry tableward. Beerlifts. Stops. Shit, I can't drink anymore. Want some coffee?

Sure. Time to quit anyways . . .

John bathroom enters. Doorshuts.

Jerry cleangathers empty and nearempty beers. At kitchen sink cupboardsearches. Finds coffeepot. Gripfumbles. Sends floorclattering. Manyparted pot makes much noise. Shit!

Regathers pot and reassembles atop stove.

Nightie-dressed and housecoated Sally stairdescends.

I heard noise.

Dropped the goddamn coffee pot.

Helpmoving-Sally to stove.

I'll do it.

No. Go to bed.

Beside him Sally-reaching. You've got this wrong . . .

GODDAMMIT!

Deadviolent moving Jerry wifegrabs. Heaves stairward. Counterslamming. Headhitting cupboard door.

Sally goes down.

Coffeepot dissembleclatters and strews.

I told you to go to bed, goddammit!

Writhing-Sally whimpercries.

Oh for fuck sake. Stop that. You always do that. Goddammit!

Starting perhaps a helpgesture Jerry halfstoops and enfolds. Tries to move her. Ends kickingsending. Terrible direction. Kickassaults. Knee and foot. Control-loss. Switches feet. Maximum awful kickpower. Face-crush. Rib-snap. Scream. Snap.

Jerry! Don't!

Shut up. (Kick.) Shut up fuckin bitch! (Kickpunch.)

Fly-furniture. Blood-fly. Sound and scream.

Bathroom-door crack-sufficient John's head to show. Assault-noise non-ignorable. Shocklistening. John observes action. Withdraws. Doorclosing with care.

Melee concludes. Panting-Jerry selfsupports at kitchen counter. Internal-injuried-Sally mouthbleeds. Softwhimpers.

Headshaking-Jerry handrubs hair. Shivers.

Look, ahh . . . You gotta go to bed.

Unsteady-Jerry overstands Sally. Armgathers across floor and labourpulls stairward. Dropplaces head upon second and third step. Stares balefully toiletward. Gentlepushes her.

Crawl, honey. C'mon.

Sally crawlbegins. Husband watches for moments. Turns. Assemblepicks coffeepot pieces. Sally away slow.

Attempt-Jerry the coffee procedure. Non-finish. Selfbegins circlewalk roundkitchen. Armwraps around. Sidepats himself. Handwrings and shakes. Smileattempts. Facepats. Remembers bathroom occupant.

Doorspeaks. Johnny. . . Havin a crap in there?

Wanders furtherseconds. Tablesits. Glum.

Bathroom door slowopens. Emergent-John. Glumlooks Jerry. Nearspeech-ready but quiet. Headshakes. Windowheads. Sighs. Armfolds and looks out.

Begin tearcrying-Jerry.

Turning-John looks Jerryward. Then back window-ward.

Jerrysobbing-heavy. Tears astream. To tabletop facelowers. Armcradles head audibleweeping.

Returning-John comes eyes floorward. To table slowwalks armunfolding. To Jerry chairdraws. Sits. Handraises but stops. Handdrops slow on Jerry's shoulderbacks. Rubpats. Gentle.

Easy, kid.

Soothecomforting-John for moments. Stops. Armlowers. Cross-stares overtable. Backleans to ceiling-gaze. Grimace. Deep-grimace. Wordmired. Talk-tries. Straightens freshfaced shaking for subjectchange.

Ever tell you. . .

Grimace. Silent-time terror.

Ever tell you about the time my little brother and me stole the railroad switch engine?

Crystopped-Jerry non-acknowledges.

Talking-John rises. Makesbusy cleanup-talking. Coffee-makes.

You might know the story already, I can't remember. We used to live near the railyard at home. I told you about that. Me and my brother used to play there on weekends. Weekends there wouldn't be anybody there cept a watch-man but he was old and drunk most of the time. We used to climb the boxcars and walk along on top, scare the shit out of each other jumping from one to another. It's awful high up there, a real surprise to somebody who's never done it . . . I musta been . . . Oh fuck . . . I musta been eleven. Stevey was eight. The yard engines were so old and decrepit they used to have so much trouble starting them they'd just leave them running all weekend. Just idling there on the track. When we were younger we were scared of the noise they made. Never went near em. As we got older we used to go closer and closer and then we used to climb on em. We used to dare each other to do it. Then one day Steve dared me to crawl inside. I did. Found out how to trip the door latch and let him in. God, what a thrill for a kid. Buttons and knobs and gauges . . . We sat both of us in the engineer's chair, pretended we were going and waving to kids. The rumble of the thing when you were inside was incredible! The power of the thing! It shook you right inside. Wasn't long before I discovered the little lever, the thing the engineer uses to drive the thing, the throttle they call it I guess on one those things . . . Anyway, it was this little lever, really small, right by the engineer's stool. You pushed it forward, the engine would rev up. Christ it scared us the first time but we got used to it . . . Yeah we got used to it. Anyway, one day we were crowding in there playing and we fought over who would monkey with the throttle and I won. So I pushed it a few times and Stevey started reaching for it too and then we were moving. Holy shit. I took my hand off the lever and the engine revved down and we stopped but were we scared. . .

Stevey scrambled for the door and I noticed he'd been crowding me so much he'd been standing on this little pedal on the floor. I found out later they call it a dead man's pedal . . . or switch or whatever. The engineer has to have his foot on the thing at all times or the engine won't run. I guess it's in case the guy has a heart attack or something . . . So, now we had the secret of how the world worked. None of our friends would believe it, of course, so it was up to Steve and me to demonstrate for em. We'd move the thing a few feet, win a few bets, pay a kid to look out for the watchman . . . It wasn't long before somebody dared us to really take the thing for a run and like fools we were game. We climbed into the cab and I pointed down the track about a quarter mile to a big tree and said we'd take it all the way there and that would be it. We started off and right away we were going faster than we'd ever gone before. A godawful screeching noise came up. I figured out later it must have been the brakes. They were on but so worn out they couldn't hold er. We were at the tree in no time but I didn't want to stop. Stevey started yelling for me to ease off but I remember I just laughed. He started screaming and saying he was going to tell Mom. I just kept laughing. Finally he jumped off the pedal and went for the door. He said he'd jump if I didn't stop. I stretched myself out, got my foot on the deadman's pedal and yelled Jump! Jump ya little jam tart. See if I care.

Well, damned if the little bastard didn't jump! The second he was gone I was so full of fear . . . Scared shitless. The lever felt horrible in my hand and I realized I was sick to my stomach of the smell in there, the diesel, the hot oil . . . I pulled back the lever, jumped off the pedal and ran for the door. But now this thing was whipping like crazy along the tracks . . . Going like hell. So fast the trees went by in a green smudge. I looked around and I was so far away I didn't even know the countryside anymore. Everything was unfamiliar. I guess, now, looking back on it, it must have been a downward grade I was on, cause that awful noisy smelly engine just kept on goin, picking up speed. I was stiff, couldn't even get it together enough to panic. I'd crawled out to the side, the wind blowing my hair back, the noise so bad I couldn't think. I knew I had to jump but I also knew I didn't have the balls. The thing was lurching and bumping so bad I had to hang on til my knuckles were numb. My time was coming, I could feel it. All the dares I'd taken, and now this. I was gonna die. Crushed like a slug. I could see the engine rolling over and over, me under, getting squished, my head squashed, all the guts out of me, my arms and legs ripped off . . . I knew I'd never drive anything again . . . I didn't want to. I just wanted it to be over.

Then . . . I guess what happened was the engine hit a

siding, changed tracks . . . The lurch sent me off into the wind. My eyes were closed. I remember floating. Next thing I knew I was running, back, along the track, toward home. Hurt, scratched, bloody . . . I just ran and ran. Ran til I got home . . .

John-voice trailoff. Windowgazes. Morninglight arriving during storytell. Jerry sleeps. John wakeshakes. Jerry evenbreathing. Sleeps.

Tottering-John unsteadily stoveward. Coffee is ready. Takes humungothermos and outswills with tapwater. Carefulfills coffee. Overslings thermos leather carrythong.

Rewakeshakes Jerry. No response. Efforting. Armprops shoulders and unseats grogged-out co-worker.

C'mon Jer. Gotta go to work . . .

Weavemaking two crossfloor. John Jerryleans through door.

Co-stagger outward.

« FOUR »

Original workplant-main lunchroom. Remember tables and benches. Candymachine. Walls loudspeaking safetyposters.

BE CAREFUL AND LIVE
SAFETY FIRST

Plantbuzzernoise long and loud. Rumbling and footfalls.

Machine winddowns. Power diminishment.

Thermosladen-John-and-Ravi slumpwalk through. Ravi with lunchbox giganti-size.

Emphatic-John. No, no . . . Forget it.

Like the crazed elephant, you strike your head against the tree.

Hah, sure sounds like some kinda nursery story when you say things like that.

Whatever. I am right am I not?

Unlunchboxing and unthermos-screwing they sit.

I think I know what you mean but you're wrong.

Maybe so. I can accept it.

You can accept it.

Yes.

Let's talk about this another time.

Gladly.

Tell you one thing, (Yawn.) you sure can work. How come we never worked together before?

Your life was not right maybe.

Heh, heh . . . You are weird. Aren't you there, hombre?

Weird is a state of mind. Desirable sometimes.

Uh huh. And I suppose it maybe helps a guy along in life. Makes work okay. Stuff like that . . .

That is possible.

Dat is possible . . .

Carl and Allen arrive to interrupt mimickidding. Sit. Unlunchbox. Roughlook Carl sports blackeye.

Closeregarding John. Jeez . . . Coming out real bright . . .

Forget it.

Sorry.

No apology necessary.

Eattalking-Allen chuckles. Heh, heh . . . I gotta make a

point of comin out for one a these tag-team matches . . .

Nothin to see, Al . . .

He's right. Cep for Ravi. He's a real star . . .

Dank-you pal.

Rodeo star.

Dancefloor star.

Ride em, Ravi! Hah, hah:

Grimacelaughing Carl. Ooo. Jaw hurts when I laugh . . .

If it's any consolation to ya, it was just a lucky shot . . .

Real lucky John, considering the load you were carrying . . .

Laugh-eat.

Staring-John thermospours. Idleswilling coffee in cup.

Concerned-Allen. No lunch?

Naw.

Want some of mine?

It's okay.

You look awful tired . . .

I am . . .

What happened to your partner this morning? First I seen im, then he was gone. . .

Went home. He's totally wasted.

Rising-John pocketsearches. Anybody got change for a five?

Yeah. . .

Carl jeansearches. Here.

Thanks.

Candymachine bars fall. Thunk-sounds herald stomping-upset Mary.

John Watkins, you are the world's biggest asshole!

What?

Intoning-Carl. Whoa, Nelly . . .

You prick.

What are you talking about?

Don't pretend. You know what I'm talking about but you're such a flying fucking jerkface you won't admit it.

Hold it. You gotta tell me what's goin on?

You took a perfectly decent, hardworking man and turned him into a quivering mess.

Who you talking about?

Who the fuck else but Jerry?

He's not quivering. He's just tired and went home.

Not before he went to Ainsley's office and quit.

Quit?

Don't pretend to be surprised.

Holy shit!

Thoughtspeaking-Allen. Looked pretty bad this morning.

You did it to him.

I didn't tell him to quit.

You didn't have to tell him. What else can a person do if they're forced to work with a drunken lazy goof who won't hold up his end and always causes trouble. I've never seen anyone so depressed and upset. He left the office crying.

He had a hard night . . .

You're not kidding and you should know shouldn't you. You, who always put a wrench into anything good around here because you hate the company so much.

Deflating-John awayturns. Take it easy . . .

I won't take it easy. I can't believe you. I can't believe you'd let that man work so hard right beside you all these years and not try to help him instead of hinder him. It just boggles my mind.

Conciliatory-Allen. Ease up, there, Mary. . . Siddown.

I can't. I think I'm gonna blow. And after he spent all last night talking to Ainsley, trying to get a better job.

Perking-Carl. Oh yeah. How'd he do?

Lousy. You can ask your friend here why.

Gimme a break, Mar . . .

The only break you should get is across your skull. What kind of a break did you give Jerry?

I tell ya I thought he was just tired and was gonna go home . . .

He went home all right. Told personnel to write his pay-out cheque. What's he going to do now? Nobody can get a job nowadays . . .

Wondrous-Allen-and-Carl.

Just up and quit, eh.

Real man of action . . .

Disgusted-Mary.

It's not funny.

Retorting-Carl. Well, I don't know about a guy who can't take the heat. I mean, if he didn't want to work with John he shoulda transferred . . .

God knows why he didn't.

It's got nothin to do with me, that's why.

Sure.

It's true . . . Look, Mary. He had a lot on his mind. I can't explain . . . Trust me.

Leavetaking-Mary. Forgive me if I find that a hard order to fill. I think I'll go and puke.

Footsteps loud amid Allen-Ravi-Carl.

He did look bad . . .

He did.

Yeah but how bad does it have to get to up and quit your job like that? Guy's got something wrong with his head.

Sitting-John. You guys don't know what you're talking about.

Silence. Lunchholders eat. Candybar-nibbler-John stares.

Quiet-breaking Allen. Somebody oughta call im or something . . .

I'll see him.

Thinking-Carl. Think it should be you?

Why not? Mary's got it wrong . . .

Even so . . .

Intervening-Ravi. Johnny is right. The man wants to talk to his friend he should do so. Friends are friends when it rains or when the sun is shining.

Maybe where you come from. But around here guys get their teeth kicked in over stuff like this.

Naw Carl. He's right.

Agreeful-Allen. Maybe. Sounds good . . .

Hmmm . . .

I'll go see im. I think I got it figured out. I'm gonna figure it out for sure. For Jerry an me, by god . . .

Juncture urgent-pierced by bellbuzzer. Alarmchime. Shortsharp wailing series panic-sounding.

John's speechramble rises through. We're gonna beat this sucker, Jerry an me. We're gonna get his job back or get another job, I dunno. . .

Startled-Carl. What the hell is that! Lunch isn't over yet!

Slapclosing-lunchbox Allen. Sumpin's wrong.

Everything's gonna be okay . . .

Whatta we do?

Everything's gonna be fine . . .

Buzzringing joined with awful roarhonking. Flashlighting.

Running-Mary upon scene. Number three machine is on fire!

Fuck!

Let's go . . .

Leave-lunch-hurried-leavetaking. All but ramble-John.

She'll be okay. Everybody's gonna be okay. I'll be okay . . . Jerry boy, you gonna be fine.

Bluespeaks.

You gonna be a fine specimen of a man, my man.

You gonna be great!

You gonna fly, boy.

You gonna git pie, in the sky, boy . . .

Da DAH da-dum.

Da DAH da-dum.

Da da dah dum.

You gonna be mine, my boy.

Da dah da-dum.

You gonna be fine.

Da dah da-dum.

Walkingbluestalking-John to candymachine.

You gonna be fine, boy.

Buttonpunches vigourous. Violent candy assault.

Da dah da-dum.

Smittenbars drop. Blues-scooped by rhythm-John.

You gonna be fine.

Plunderrips candypaper. Bites defiant sugar-shot teeth-held in joy-contempt. Gothic-dark plant. Smokeroom glowlighting. Electro-shorted pyroscenario. Fright. End. Fumebound John dance-eats. Pirouettes.

Da dah da-dum . . .

Buzzhorror anger-drones.

Dance-eating-John coughs. Humming ramble.

Fadelights in smokewrangle. John-voice moiled. Dashfleet to and about. Flutter-touch in dysphoria-unended.

ABOUT THE AUTHOR

Since his first highly-acclaimed 1992 novel, *Stupid Crimes*, DENNIS E. BOLEN has written two other novels: *Stand In Hell* and *Krekshuns.* For many years Mr. Bolen has held the post of Fiction Editor for the literary journal *sub-TERRAIN,* and has served as a contributing editor to the *Vancouver Review*, and part-time editorial board member at the *Vancouver Sun*. He is currently working on a new novel, *Toy Gun*.

For a free catalogue of Anvil Press books, write to:

Anvil Press Publishers
#204-A 175 East Broadway,
Vancouver, B.C. V5T 1W2
CANADA